Christian Black, Esq.

A "Holy Rock Chronicles" Short

Shelia Writes Books

Perfect Stories About Imperfect People Like You...and Me!

SCANLIFE

Get more Info About Shelia E. Bell books!

Perfect Stories About Imperfect People Like You...and Me!

Christian Black, Esq.

A "Holy Rock Chronicles" Short

Shelia Writes Books

Perfect Stories About Imperfect People Like You...and Me!

National Bestselling Author

Shelia E. Bell

"Holy Rock Chronicles" is a captivating spinoff series of short stories that take you on a journey into the intriguing lives of the notorious members of the Graham and McCoy families from the national bestselling "My Son's Wife" series. These *shorts* are specially crafted to provide an exclusive, behind-the-scenes look at the characters' lives while I continue to pen the next thrilling installment in this captivating family saga.

I am grateful for your continued support and for choosing to read my work! Thank you!

Acknowledgements

I cannot thank my readers enough for your loyalty, dedication, and encouragement, which have played a vital role in shaping my writing career. Thank you for being part of my journey. You are invaluable and I am truly blessed to have such amazing people in my life. Your passion for my work is what motivates me to strive for excellence, and I could not have come this far without your support over the years. I am also grateful for all the individuals whom God has placed in my life to guide and support me, and for removing those who may have hindered my progress. I thank God for the gift of imagination and the determination to continue writing, even during moments of self-doubt. Your support and unwavering belief in me have been instrumental in helping me stay on track towards fulfilling my purpose. Rest assured, I will continue to deliver the best stories I can, and I am excited to share many more exciting literary adventures with you in the future.

Shelia E. Bell
God's Amazing Girl

one

"Every new beginning comes from some other beginning's end." Seneca

It was the ideal beginning to the perfect Sunday. The autumn sun had risen slowly, casting a magnificent golden glow on the sky, while fluffy white clouds floated lazily by.

"You ready?" Christian swallowed the last of his coffee, followed up with a bite of his strawberry bagel.

"Yes, I'm coming." Luna traipsed down the winding stairs of their luxurious home.

Christian stuffed another piece of bagel into his mouth while standing in front of the floor-to-ceiling windows of their family room. He marveled at the massive black walnut tree swaying gracefully in the breeze. Its leaves, rustling together in perfect harmony as they skipped across their professionally landscaped front yard, reminded him he was a far cry from the nonstop chaos of New York City.

The five months they had been in Tennessee, the slower pace of southern living was proving to be a refreshing change, and Christian savored every moment.

Luna appeared from behind, slightly startling him. "Honey, why would you eat that now? You should have eaten before you got dressed. You know you can be like a kid when it comes to spilling food on your clothes."

Christian quickly popped the last bit of bagel into his mouth. He turned toward Luna, smiled, pecked her on the cheek, and walked ahead of her to the garage entrance. "No worries, I didn't waste any this time. Come on, let's get out of here."

Entering the large space, Luna went and stood between their cars. Eyeing each vehicle she said, "Yours or mine?"

"Yours," Christian replied, strolling up to his wife's car.

"Okay, but you're still driving."

"As if I didn't already know." Christian chuckled, opened the door, allowing her to get inside and seated before going around to the driver's side.

"Where to first?" he asked, taking a glance at the clock on the dash.

"Um, let's stick to our plans and go to Holy Rock first. I know we're leaving home a little later than usual, but we can still make it in time for the nine-thirty service. After we leave there, we'll head to *New* Holy Rock."

"Sounds like a plan," replied Christian.

Luna smoothed the hem of her dress with her hands and then looked inside her purse, removing a small designer compact. Opening it,

2

she gazed at her reflection in the mirror. She used her tongue to remove any lingering lipstick from her teeth, and then gently closed the compact and placed it back inside her purse.

"You know, bae, we've been doing this since we moved to Memphis." Christian sighed and gripped the steering wheel. "I'm ready to decide on a church home," he said, as he looked both ways before pulling out of their driveway.

"Okay, I understand we've been visiting quite a few churches, honey, but I don't want to rush anything. I want us to be comfortable and feel accepted wherever we decide to join. I don't want to church hop. I want to work in a ministry, maybe a children's or women's ministry." Tugging gently on his suit jacket, she said, "Anyway, it seems like we've narrowed it down to either Holy Rock or New Holy Rock. They're the two we've visited the most."

"I'm just saying, after today, I'd like us to make a decision. For me, it's New Holy Rock," Christian said.

"I'm not surprised." Luna shrugged and turned up her lips. "If I had to choose right now, I would choose Holy Rock. They have a ton of ministries and they do so much in the community and for the city," Luna said, reaching over and affectionately kneading Christian's free hand.

Christian looked over his shoulder to make sure the road was clear. He steered the car into the far right lane and drove toward the merging lane leading to I-240.

"Don't get me wrong; I enjoy both Pastor Stiles *and* Pastor Khalil, but I like Pastor Khalil's preaching style a bit more. Plus, Holy Rock has a more diverse congregation *and* three services we can choose to attend. New Holy Rock is, well, think about it, they already have a lot of drama going on."

"Drama? I don't follow you."

Luna gave him an awkward look. "Uhh, their senior pastor is serving twelve years in prison. That's enough drama in and of itself. You're his attorney. What is it going to look like for you to be part of that congregation? I don't know, Christian. The man has a felony record and two ex-wives under his belt. Can you really sit under the leadership of someone like that? Do you expect me to?"

"What does his past have to do with where we join? If they preach and teach the Word, then that's all that should matter," Christian said. "And I guess you forgot it's his brother whose the pastor, not my client."

"I know that." Luna sighed and scrunched her shoulders. "Still, it just doesn't look right, especially for a senior pastor. Don't get me wrong, I do like Pastor Stiles. I think he's a good pastor, but remember, he's only the interim pastor. On a positive note, it *does* have a ministry or two that I could probably join."

"Remember it's a smaller congregation than Holy Rock, so it's not expected they would have all the ministries and outreach programs like his son's church," Christian added.

"That's true, but at Holy Rock we could meet a lot of people, make a lot of connections. I think that would be great, especially for you."

"You're right; I can see your point," Christian said.

Upon arriving at Holy Rock, they found a parking space on the street after seeing a PARKING LOT FULL sign blocking the entrance to the huge church.

"Well, one thing we know about Holy Rock is if we want to park on the lot we have to arrive early," said Christian, parallel parking the Acura.

Christian got out of the car and opened his wife's door.

Luna grabbed her purse and got out. "We have a long walk. I don't like this."

"Look at the bright side; we'll get some of our daily steps in." Christian smiled and wrapped an arm around his wife's waist as they walked along the sidewalk leading to one of the multiple church entrances.

Royal purple carpet and purple cloth covered pews accentuated the divine beauty of Holy Rock. Different styles of paintings of Christ and other Christian symbols hung strategically throughout the massive sanctuary.

"This really *is* a beautiful place of worship," Luna whispered, looking around, as they followed the crowd into the sanctuary.

"You say that every time we come here," Christian remarked.

"Because it's true." Strolling hand in hand, Luna gasped. The sanctuary was filling up fast. The balcony extended around the whole upper portion of the church, and there were people quickly filling those seats as well.

"I'm glad we got a seat down here. I wasn't looking forward to sitting in the balcony again," Luna leaned in and whispered.

"Neither was I," Christian agreed.

The two of them looked toward the front of the sanctuary as a booming voice approached the pulpit proclaiming, "This is the day the Lord has made." The voice poured from an average height man with a fair complexion and a stocky build, attired in a chocolate brown suit that appeared to be at least one size too large, and hung loosely even on his heavy frame.

"We will rejoice and be glad in it," much of the congregation bellowed, including Luna and Christian.

When the man finished his prayer and scripture reading, majestic purple curtains cascaded down from the top of the sanctuary, opening wide to unveil Holy Rock's award-winning choir.

Luna rejoiced, raising her hands in praise, singing along with the choir as the words to the songs appeared on projectors hanging on each side of the towering sanctuary walls.

Christian was more subtle with his praise. While Luna stood to her feet, he remained seated and nodded his head as he sang along.

Pastor Khalil appeared from the front side entrance and charismatically walked to the pulpit as the choir proceeded to sing the last stanza of their third song.

"Praise the Lord," Khalil said and started singing the song again, revitalizing the choir and the congregation as he strolled across the pulpit performing like he was a *Kirk Franklin* clone.

two

"Each day is a new beginning, the chance to do with it what should be done, and not to be seen as simply another day to put in the time." C. Pulsifer

"I liked Pastor Khalil's message and how he delivered it. He's a bit theatrical, but he still preaches the word. He may be young in the ministry but he preaches like someone much older. And boy can he sing! He certainly has charm and the ability to draw people into what he's saying," Luna said as they left Holy Rock.

"That's obvious from the packed sanctuary. I like that he has a livestream on Sundays and a podcast a couple times a week. It shows he's keeping up with the times and doing what it takes to reach people whether they are physically in the church or watching online," said Christian.

"Right." Luna nodded. "Oh, and the choir, oh my gosh, they are phenomenal." Luna placed her hand across her heart, shaking her head and exhaling.

"Yep, I enjoyed them too," added Christian, approaching the interstate and headed toward New Holy Rock.

Fifteen minutes after leaving Holy Rock they arrived at New Holy Rock.

"One thing I like about New Holy Rock is not having to walk a mile," said Luna, holding on to her husband's hand as they made their way to the entrance. "A check for convenient parking." Luna made a checkmark gesture in the air.

Christian chuckled. He held the door open for Luna as they climbed the final step.

They easily found a seat inside the sanctuary. Moments later the service started.

The more he heard Stiles preach, the more Christian felt a spiritual draw to the man. Today's message was a powerful word about relationships and God's perfect timing. Christian had learned over the years, mostly because of his dear wife, not to fight against his spirit. Luna was always talking about how the Holy Spirit operated and that people should take time to listen to their spirits more often.

At the end of New Holy Rock's 90-minute service, Luna and Christian stood in line with other congregants so they could say hello to Pastor Stiles.

Moving along in the line, and almost instinctively, Christian placed his arm affectionately at the center of his wife's back and kissed her on top of her head. She looked up at him and smiled.

"It was nice to see the two of you again in the congregation this morning," Stiles said when Christian and Luna approached.

"Thank you, we enjoyed the service, as always," Christian responded.

"Your message was right on time," Luna followed, reaching out to meet Stiles' extended hand.

"Thank you, Sista Black."

After Luna's handshake, Christian extended his hand towards Stiles for a cordial exchange between the two gentlemen.

"Yes, I agree with my wife. Your sermon was definitely on point."

"Thank you. I wish I could take credit, but it's all God," Stiles replied. "My question to the two of you is when are you going to become part of our ministry? We'd love to have you, and I know my brother would love to hear news that his attorney joined his church." Stiles shared a charming smile as he spoke.

Christian chuckled and looked at Luna, but did not verbally reply.

"We're praying on it," Luna spoke up.

"Yes, we're seeking God's direction," added Christian.

"I can't do anything but respect that. Let God direct you. Look, let's get together or talk later this week, Brother Black," Stiles offered. "That is, if you have time. I know you're a busy man. I'd like to talk about my brother's case, if that's okay."

One of the deacons whispered something to Stiles. Stiles looked to his left briefly at the line of people still waiting to greet him.

"Look, let's talk this week," he said, rapidly shaking Christian and Luna's hands again.

"Okay, I'll have my administrative assistant call and set something up," Christian suggested and the couple walked off.

three

"Change can be scary, but you know what's scarier? Allowing fear to stop you from growing, evolving, and progressing." Mandy Hale

The following week, Christian and Stiles met for lunch at Christian's office. Christian ordered a barbeque spread complete with chopped shoulder, baked beans, slaw and a gallon of sweet tea. During the meeting, Christian collected more information about Hezekiah's family and background. There was a lot to unpack and Christian was ready for the journey.

Christian rested back in his office chair, listening to Stiles, while eating.

"I just want my brother out of there. He's innocent. Attorney Whitfield knew that. He worked hard for my brother, but obviously it wasn't good enough because Hezekiah is upstate behind steel bars. I hated to learn about Whitfield's illness, but I thank God Hezekiah has you now. God is good. Yes, he is." Stiles sighed.

"I've still been going through his files. I came across some things I have yet to talk to your brother about."

"Because of the recent lockdown?"

"Exactly—and phone calls just don't work. I need to sit across from him and be able to listen to what he has to say. I need to learn more about his ex-wife, or I should say his ex-*wives*," Christian emphasized, swiveling around to face his computer. "Starting with whatever you can tell me about Rianna McCoy. If you think she had something to do with him being sent to prison, I definitely need to know."

"Sure, whatever I can tell you, I will."

"First, tell me about the relationship between you and your brother. You said earlier that you didn't know about each other until a few years ago. How did that come about?"

Stiles recounted the story of him and Hezekiah, including the details of their birth mother Margaret and her connection to Audrey Graham, Margaret's half-sister.

"Margaret gave Hezekiah to a woman on a Greyhound bus when he was a baby. Audrey took me from Margaret when I was a toddler and raised me as her own son by claiming Margaret was mentally unstable. My birth mother is responsible for a rampage at Holy Rock that's known as the Jubilee Tragedy. She killed seven people that Sunday." Stiles bowed his head, shaking it in disgust.

Christian was amazed as he listened to the unbelievable tale of how the two brothers had come to meet.

13

The meeting lasted for almost two hours before Christian's administrative assistant buzzed his office.

"Attorney Black, your two-thirty has arrived."

"Thank you, Beverly. Tell them I'll be right with them."

Both men rose from their seats. "Well, thank you for lunch," Stiles said. "I see you've already learned you can never go wrong with Memphis barbeque."

The men chuckled and Christian walked from around his desk and extended his hand toward Stiles. "Oh, there's something I forgot to ask."

"What's that?"

"Have you heard of a Horace and Felicia McKellar?"

Stiles seemed to tense up and his eyes slightly bulged. "Umm, no, I can't say that I have. Who are they?"

"Look, it's nothing we can't talk about later," Christian said. "I need to see my next client. We'll talk later this week."

"Ok, sounds good."

Christian opened his door and Stiles exited. "Come in, Mr. and Mrs. Brady," he greeted his next clients as Stiles walked away.

†

Luna, along with one of her direct reports, returned to her office from an afternoon meeting.

"That was a long but productive meeting," Luna said as she and Gregory sat at a round table in the corner of her office suite. The various blue hues decorating the space made it a welcoming environment. It felt more like a sanctuary rather than an office. From soft cerulean blue to cobalt blue, the blends and artistic designs of the modern table and ergonomically designed chairs, to the durable deep carpeted tile floor, all made for a good feel. Her office view, unlike Christian's, was not of the river, but she still enjoyed a large, secluded office where she could see parts of downtown.

"I think it was positive, too. I'm glad they are pleased with our services. We only stand to keep improving."

"I agree, Gregory. You have the ability to see the bigger picture. I see why you are Director of Product Development."

"Thank you," her direct report said, blushing. His hazel eyes seemed to sparkle when he displayed a smile that showed his teeth and gumline. Pushing back a lock of reddish-blonde hair from his face, he said, "If you don't have anything else, I'm going to head to my office."

"Of course, go ahead; we're done."

"Thanks," he said, pushing back from the table and rising. "Oh, I'll be leaving early today. It's my day to pick up Junie from soccer practice."

"Okay, no problem. I'll probably be here a little late this evening."

"Late? Why is that? Is there something I can help you with?"

"No, nothing like that," Luna said, flippantly throwing up a hand and rising from her chair. "I just have some things I need to finish up, reports to be read, emails to respond to, that sort of thing."

"Okay, well, I'll see you in the morning."

"Bye, Gregory."

"Hold my calls, please," she told her assistant and closed her office door. Returning to the round table and sitting, she stared at the mother and child painting gracing the wall across from the table. It was a special piece, close to her heart because she bought it the summer she and Christian toured France. The painting held bits of her favorite color—blue. It took her to a place today where she became somewhat melancholy. Usually it made her smile, but today it made her think about her reality. That reality was not giving birth to a child of her own. It wasn't Christian's fault, she understood that, but it didn't keep her from desiring to feel life growing inside her belly. She would never experience that. She and Christian talked about adoption, which she wasn't against, but it wasn't the same as carrying a child made in love for nine months and birthing that child into the world.

Tears formed but she quickly wiped them away, looking around the office as if expecting to see a roomful of people staring at her like she was crazy. *Stop it, Luna. You're blessed, girl. God has been good to you. You have a man who adores you, people who love you, a great career, a beautiful home, and friends. Okay, so because of Christian's sterility you can't have a kid the natural way. Don't blame him. You knew his condition before you married him and you accepted that. Don't go acting all upset about it now.* She continued her mental conversation until the sound of Christian's ringtone brought her back to the present.

"Hey, sweetheart," she said, displaying a big smile when she heard his voice.

"Hey, there. Busy?"

"No, I just came out of a meeting. I was sitting here reflecting on some things. What's up?"

"I just had my last meeting. How much longer will you be at the office? I was thinking we could meet for dinner downtown. Maybe on Beale," he suggested.

"I wish I could," she sighed, "but I won't be leaving until later tonight. I might as well tell you now that I'll be working late the remainder of the week. We have some new clients. I also have a couple other projects I'm trying to bring to a close. I'm sorry, babe," she cooed.

"Nah, I understand. It's part of having a big shot executive for a wife," he lovingly teased. "You want me to bring you something to eat up there? Or I can order something to be delivered."

"Not right now. Doesn't the game come on tonight? I know you want to watch it."

"Yeah, it does."

"Okay, well why don't you order yourself a pizza or something. I'll order something later if I get hungry. Plus, you know I keep snacks and diet soda in my office," she said, laughing.

Christian chuckled into the phone. "Yeah, I know. Well, call me later if your plans change. I'm about to leave the office. Since you can't do dinner, I'm going to call and see if my barber can chop me up real quick. If he can, then that's where I'm headed first. On the way home, I'll stop and get a pizza or something before the game comes on."

"Okay, that sounds good, sweetie. I love you. I'll call or text you when I'm on my way home."

"Okay, love you, too."

four

"If you're brave enough to say goodbye, life will reward you with a new hello." Paulo Coelho

Christian arrived home and placed his large pepperoni and jalapeno pizza with extra cheese on top of the quartz kitchen island. After that, he headed for the bathroom. It was during times like these, when the house was empty, that he thought of how much he longed to be a father. The mere thought of hearing the pitter-patter of little feet running around filled him with joy. He imagined Luna's voice, yelling lovingly at the kids to quiet down. He envisioned coming home from a long day at the office to the warm welcome of children happy to see him. The thought made him laugh out loud, but the longing in his heart remained.

Christian and Luna had discussed the possibility of adoption several times, but they had yet to take action. Now that they were comfortably settled into their new careers, they had agreed to move forward and start the process. Despite this, Christian couldn't shake the feeling that Luna longed to have biological children. Unfortunately, this was a gift he could never give her, and it weighed heavily on his heart.

Dispelling the bothersome thoughts, he posed in front of the bathroom mirror, studied his fresh cut, then started to disrobe in preparation for a shower.

After freshening up with a rejuvenating shower, he donned a cozy pair of plaid pajama bottoms. Soft suede slippers enveloped his feet in comfort as he made his way to the spacious chef-style kitchen. He warmed his pizza and poured himself a tall, cold glass of lemonade and took it into the family room.

Sitting in his two-seat recliner, he reached on the side, pulled out a built-in tray, and set his food on it. Leaning back, he pushed the recliner's remote and his feet begin to slowly rise. When he got to the perfect position, he reached for the TV remote on his opposite side, turned on the projector-sized television, and switched to the football game. He relaxed and enjoyed the game. Neither team was his favorite. That's why his mind probably so easily went to thoughts of Hezekiah McCoy.

When he stumbled on Hezekiah's alias, he contacted Hezekiah's former lawyer, Thomas Whitfield. Whitfield invited Christian to come talk to him face-to-face. The lawyer was still able to talk, not without struggling, but clear enough for Christian to make out what he was saying. Hezekiah felt empathy for him; it had to be hard and quite life changing to be diagnosed with ALS, especially being a middle-aged man with a wife and kids.

By the end of the twenty-minute meeting, Christian learned Hezekiah and his first ex-wife had indeed changed their names. If they had gone so far as to have their names changed, what other secrets might the couple possibly be harboring?

Christian was scheduled to make another trip to see Hezekiah in two weeks. He had been working on a loophole he thought he may have come across during his research of cases similar to Hezekiah's. If it panned out, he was certain he could get Hezekiah released.

Next, he went to thoughts he had about his biological father. He hadn't had the opportunity to question Hezekiah to see if he possibly knew his mother from back in the day. It looked like they may have attended the same high school or possibly lived in the same neighborhood at some time or other. If it turned out Hezekiah knew his mother or her family, then there could be no telling what else he might be able to tell Christian about his mother, and who knows, maybe even about his father. *Then again,* he told himself, *if my own mother didn't know my father, how can I expect some stranger to know?* He dismissed the invasive thoughts and returned his focus to the game, screaming and raising a fist in the air when the team made a touchdown. "*Yesss!*"

†

Luna eyed her Apple watch. "Dang. Seven o'clock already? I have to get out of here. I wasn't planning on staying this late."

Luna headed toward the elevator, noticing everybody on her floor had already left, except for another associate she saw in his office on the phone.

Getting off the elevator, the clickety-clack of her red-bottom pumps against the concrete pavement sounded almost musical when she started the short trek to her car. Hearing an unfamiliar sound, which she thought sounded like a scream, she looked around the deserted garage, seeing other cars but not another human in sight. The hair on the back of her neck stood up; her heart began to slightly race.

Luna had heard more than her share of horror stories about crime in Memphis. The local news was saturated with one story after another, on a daily basis. She picked up her pace and started rummaging in her purse for her keys as she walked. Christian always fussed about her waiting until the last minute to retrieve her keys, especially when she was out like this, alone.

She stuck a hand inside her blazer pocket and sighed when she felt them. Her heart raced as she struggled with the keys, her hands lightly trembling. For what reason, she didn't know. She looked around again. Again, no one was in sight. "Girl, stop being so paranoid," she said aloud.

She opened the car door, shaking her head in disbelief for acting so weird. She scanned the eerie garage for any signs of danger, her senses still on high alert. Although she saw no one, she heard a car door closing nearby, followed by daunting footsteps that seemed to be drawing closer.

She looked around again. This time she saw a man in a black overcoat with a hat pulled down over his head, making it hard to see his face. He wore dark shades. He had one hand in his coat pocket. With lightning-fast reflexes, she darted inside her car, slamming the door shut with a loud thud. She frantically pressed the lock button, her heart pounding in her chest. She could feel her breath coming in short gasps as she leaned back against the seat, trying to calm down before starting the engine.

With a shake of her head, she turned the ignition, her mind still racing from the adrenaline rush.

Headlights suddenly appeared, casting a blinding glare into the garage and keeping her frozen in her space. She looked to her left and saw the man again. He was coming towards her car. She inhaled and gripped the steering wheel. She sighed heavily when he walked past and headed to the garage elevator.

Luna watched the man press the elevator button and step inside. The car she'd seen had approached and passed her vehicle. She breathed a sigh of relief, realizing that she had allowed her fear to get the best of her for no apparent reason.

"You are such a drama queen," she said aloud, laughing. Safely out of the garage, she called Christian when she was caught at the traffic light. "Baby," she said when Christian answered, "I just left the office, I'm on my way home. Do I need to stop and pick up anything? Did you eat?"

"Yep, I ate. I text and told you there's some left."

She pulled her phone back from her ear and looked at her text messages. Christian had texted her almost an hour ago.

"Oh, I see the text. I'll eat the leftover pizza," Luna said. "I'll stop by Zaxby's and pick up a salad to go with it."

"Okay, I'll see you in a bit."

"Okay, babe," Luna replied and ended the call.

Her phone rang almost as soon as the call ended with Christian. Looking at the screen, she saw it was Tiffany Hayes, a lady she'd met recently at work. Tiffany worked on the fourth floor and was vice-president of HR. The two women hit it off and had gone to lunch a couple of times and would talk or text a few times a week.

"Hey, Tiffany. How are you?"

"I'm good. I was calling to apologize for having to skip out on lunch. That retention project is becoming more of a headache than I anticipated. How was your day?"

"Thank goodness it's officially ended. I'm leaving the office. I had," and still have," she emphasized, "a ton of work, but I had to get out of there today. I'm still learning the ends and outs of this position. I love it but it's just a lot more to adapt to."

"I understand. Well, I was calling to see if you might be interested in going to this play with me this weekend. Hubby's job gave him two complimentary tickets, but he already had plans to go camping with the boys. Not that he wanted to go anyway. He says it's one of those chick flick plays." Tiffany laughed.

Laughing too, Luna said, "Okay, I might take you up on that. Let me check with Christian first to make sure he doesn't have anything special planned for us. If he doesn't, then I'll be glad to go. I'll text you and let you know later."

"Okay, talk to you later."

"Buh-bye." Luna ended the call. Minutes later, she pulled into Zaxby's drive through.

five

"The beginning is always today." Mary Shelley

Luna welcomed her husband's touch and reveled in his lovemaking. When they were both satisfied and spent, they remained snuggled in each other's arms. "Ummm, that was good."

"What are you talking about? The pizza or the salad?" queried Christian laughing slightly and switching from laying on his back to turning toward Luna.

"No, silly." Easing her bottom against his bareness, she playfully tapped him on his hairy chest.

"Uhh, ok so what could you possibly be talking about?" Christian teased, pulled her into him, and moved his mouth over hers before she could answer. "Could it be this?" He buried his face in her neck while using his hands to touch her in all the places he knew that turned her on. "Perhaps it was this," he hungrily moaned and so did she. "Or this."

"I love you," she said, placing butterfly kisses on his chest, glad he couldn't read the thoughts rushing through her mind about the two of them making a baby. More often than usual, baby thoughts seemed to creep up after they made love. It was becoming difficult to hold back her emotions, but she had to, for Christian's sake.

"What's wrong?" he asked as if he could sense she was bothered about something. "Everything okay at work?"

"Nothing's wrong, and everything's fine at work. Granted, it's an adjustment period. The whole move I guess has started to take a toll." Luna lifted her head toward Christian.

"Are you sorry you accepted the position?"

"No, that's not it. It's nothing, honey. Let's not talk about work. I just want to lay right here, underneath you."

Christian pushed aside his troubling thoughts and concentrated on comforting his wife. He twirled locks of Luna's hair between his fingers and leaned down and kissed the top of her head. "You do know you can talk to me about anything. Right?"

Luna looked up at him and snuggled closer. "Yeah, I know. Do you?"

"What? Do I know I can talk to my wife about anything? Sure I do." Christian said the words but he knew they were a lie as he spoke them. He would never be able to tell Luna about his moment of indiscretion. Although, it had happened years before, every now and again his mind revisited that mistake. He would never want to hurt Luna, which is why he every day he tried to prove to her how much he loved her. But of all the women he could have cheated with, why did it have to turn out to be her sister? How crazy was that? Yet, it had happened, and there was nothing he could do about it. He shook his head swiftly from side to side as if trying to shake out all the negative thoughts.

"Both of us are good then," Luna said as a yawn escaped through her lips.

He kissed her again. "Go to sleep. Sweet dreams."

†

Two days later, Christian made the five-hour drive to Bledsoe Correctional Facility. He'd been notified the previous afternoon that the lockdown had been lifted.

Driving along the prairie lined stretch of highway put him in his thoughts. He passed pasture after pasture and then ventured upon rows of solar panels lining a vast open space that went on for miles. The hills of Tennessee grew more massive in some places and barely noticeable in others. Along the drive was a small city here and there.

The South was nothing like New York. He could understand the culture shock Luna must be feeling because he felt a bit of it too.

The 2,500 acre prison was strategically, and in his estimation, purposely built on top of the

Cumberland Plateau. It sure made it harder for inmates to escape. If they managed to get past the miles of thick rows of razor edge barbwire, they would still have some of the largest stretches of forest in this part of Tennessee to get through.

Needless to say, the drive was one, especially driven alone, that put him in a melancholy mood that swiftly shifted to anger after invading thoughts about his biological father suddenly resurfaced. Why the certain need to find out who the man was? Christian had begun to question his own reasoning and sanity. Why couldn't he let it go? Millions of kids were growing up every day without a father in the home. Some of those same kids turned out just like him—successful and not missing a beat. He chastised himself for the way he was thinking.

"God, help me to be more grateful and appreciative for what you've already done in my life, what you are doing in my life, and what you are going to do." He mouthed the prayer and then quickly his thoughts fell back on his father.

"Leave it alone, man. Why can't you just let the past stay in the past. What does it matter now anyway?" He scolded himself to force himself out of the unhealthy thoughts. Next, he tapped the button on his steering wheel until he came to the new gospel playlist he'd uploaded a few days prior. Almost right away, the first song that came on ushered him into a spiritual place.

One song after another took him away from his momentary troubles and into a space of peace and contentment. Gigantic trees, mountainous hills, and endless miles of land now looked glorious and enchanting rather than boring and depressing.

As he made his way towards the towering structure of Bledsoe, a wave of calm washed over him. His thoughts drifted to the tender moments shared with Luna, his proudest career accomplishments, and the countless gifts life had bestowed upon him. Before he could fully appreciate the beauty of the surroundings, he had instinctively guided his vehicle to the grand entrance of Bledsoe.

With his signature confident stride, he emerged from his car and strode towards the prison, adhering to protocol with the practiced ease of a seasoned professional who'd made such a trip many times before. Once inside, he was directed to a private room for his meeting with Hezekiah.

After exchanging initial pleasantries, Christian and Hezekiah got down to the official reason for his visit.

Today Christian was determined to address the pressing matters at hand.

"When I was going through your files I saw you have an alias—Horace McKellar. I'm interested to hear about that. All of your latest legal cases and information bring up Hezekiah McCoy. It's like this McKellar fellow went ghost—without a trace after he served a prison stint in Chicago." Christian's eyebrows lifted. He was eager to hear what Hezekiah had to say. He'd already learned quickly that McCoy was a fast talker with the gift of gab. He wasn't surprised the man was a preacher.

"In a way, I guess you can say that's exactly what happened. Horace McKellar was my given name, but why should that matter? One thing has nothing to do with the other. Didn't Attorney Whitfield fill you in on all of that before he left?" Hezekiah's brow was etched with a deep furrow, creating a distinct crease that sliced across his forehead. The veins in his neck throbbed with the rapid pulse of his heightened state of agitation, betraying his inner turmoil.

"I want to know the reason behind it. I mean, you *are* a felon," Christian expressed. "It's hard, if not downright impossible, for a convicted felon to get a legal name change. I'm curious. How did you pull it off?"

"Let's just say, at the time I had friends in high places who made sure I didn't experience any hiccups. The reason for the change should be obvious—I didn't want that dark cloud hovering over me everywhere I went. I served my time. God forgave me for my crime. He called me to do a new thing, so I did. You should know, even though it's possible to change names in a growing number of states, some states don't keep your criminal history from being officially reported. Depends on the crime committed. I was blessed. That's the only way I can describe it. Right now I'm trying to clear Hezekiah McCoy's good name." Hezekiah appeared flustered and a bead of sweat appeared above his eyebrows, although the room was quite cold. "What I'm telling you is I started brand new, new name, new city, new state, the whole shebang. After I moved my family from Chicago to Memphis, God kept showing me favor. I knew I was where he wanted me to be. But you know, some folks get jealous when God opens doors for someone other than them. So, Attorney Black, there you have it."

Christian nodded. "You know, speaking of Chicago, that's where I'm from."

"Is that right?"

"My mother grew up near Cabrini Green, the old housing project. You know anything about it?"

"Who doesn't know about that place. I lived there for a minute and went to Cabrini High," he paused, "before dropping out in ninth grade.

Wasn't for me. It was bittersweet though when they tore Cabrini down."

"And your wife?"

"At present, I don't have a wife. Had two, which one are you talking about?" Hezekiah replied with a lopsided grin.

"Fancy McCoy *aka* Felicia McKellar. Tell me about her."

Hezekiah furrowed his eyebrows and curled his lips upwards. "She served the same amount of time that I did. That's that. She's a good girl. Always has been." He spoke slowly, clearing his throat of rumbling phlegm. "None of it was her fault; it was all me." Hezekiah's eyes glinted under the dimly lit room. "But look, let me make something clear."

"What's that?" remarked Christian.

"Whitfield knew to keep my past in the past. I hope he told you to do the same. No need for our former names to be brought up."

"Only if absolutely necessary," Christian said. "Let's talk about your sons."

"What about my sons?" Hezekiah growled.

"What kind of relationship do you have with them?"

"That oldest boy is a traitor if I ever saw one. I'm ashamed to call him my son sometimes. His mother says we butt heads because he's a lot like me. I say that might be true, but I don't betray family. He not only stole from me, he stole Holy Rock from under me too. Tried to have me sent to prison. But it's all good because New Holy Rock is not to be stopped. *I'm* not to be stopped," he said, poking his own chest. "I know God has his hands on me. He's going to get me out of here real soon. You're going to see to that or else he wouldn't have sent you," Hezekiah boldly stated and stared at Christian.

"I'm doing my best. Look, do you mind if I ask you something personal, at least it's personal for me. It's about, well about my mother."

Hezekiah nodded. "Your mother? What about your mother?"

"She's no longer living. I'm trying to find some things she left undone."

"I'm sorry. What's her name?"

"Caresha...Caresha Perkins. Back then she said most everyone called her Carrie."

Hezekiah shrugged. "Caresha? Carrie? Nah, I can't say I remember anybody back then by that name. Then again, I wasn't taking down names and keeping track, you know what I mean. I was a wild one back in my day." Hezekiah gave a short laugh.

"What about a guy named Frankie or Bae-bruh. I don't know their last names. They may have gone to the same high school as you and my mama."

Hezekiah shook his head again. "Ummm, Frankie? Bae-Bruh? No last names or real names?"

Christian shook his head. "No, that's all I know."

"Sorry, I wish I could help you." Hezekiah massaged his graying, full bearded chin.

"Thanks anyway," Christian replied.

"No problem."

"Look," Christian began gathering his folder and powering down his laptop, "I have everything I need. I'll draw up the papers and get them submitted to the high court. Whitfield was looking into using the Cosby defense. It won't work in your case. Also, I saw in your files where he overlooked quite a few substantial findings that could very well work in your favor. I'm going to use his illness in your case too. Hopefully it'll work *for* you instead of against you. In the meantime, I'll petition the high court to release you on a bond or house arrest until you go to trial or until a new ruling comes down for your permanent release."

"Sounds impressive. I hope you can pull it off," Hezekiah said, rising from his chair along with Christian. "I'll be sending up a prayer."

"I've won tougher cases. Well, I plan to see you again in a few weeks. I want to get out of here before traffic hits."

Christian shook his client's hand and confidently strolled toward the triple thick steel EXIT door.

When he left the prison an hour and a half later, he was in good spirits. He had a productive visit that gave him ammunition he needed to hopefully see Hezekiah set free in what could be a matter of months if everything went as he hoped. He was disappointed, however, to hear Hezekiah say he didn't know his mother or the men who might possibly be a connection to Christian's father.

Exiting the prison parking lot, he called Luna, but got her voicemail. Looking at his dash, he said aloud, "Must be in a meeting."

He continued his drive down I-40, mentally replaying his visit. Half an hour into the drive, he took the exit that displayed GAS and FOOD. First, he got gas. Next, he rode down the street passing a string of restaurants.

"Ummm, let's see...what do I want? Mexican? A burger? Seafood? Guess I'll have a burger. Less messy while I'm driving," he talked to himself.

"Welcome to Carl's Jr. How may I help you?" a pleasant sounding young lady asked.

"Yes, I'd like the Big Carl combo. Upsize the fries and soda please."

The server repeated the order and then instructed Christian, "Please drive to the next window for your order."

After receiving his food, he got back on the interstate. His phone rang shortly thereafter, the ringtone indicating it was Luna.

"Hey, there."

"Hi, honey. You on the road?"

"Yes, I just got back on the road. I stopped and got gas and something to eat."

"Good. How was your visit?"

"Good in some ways and disappointing in others. I'll tell you about it when I get there. Where are you? I called you earlier."

"Yes, I know. I had back-to-back meetings, and I'm still holding interviews for my direct report positions."

"How many more do you have to fill?"

"Three. I released two of my predecessor's direct reports. They didn't share my vision for the forward movement of this company."

"I heard that. You do your thang, girl," Christian flirted. "I love it when you get all sassy and feisty."

"Boy, please." Luna giggled into the phone. "Anyway, I said all of that just to remind you again I'll be getting home later than usual. Some of these interviews don't take place until after the candidates get off work. I want to be flexible as possible."

"Because that's the kind of wonderful woman and executive you are."

"I hate that you'll have to fend for yourself again," she said in a whiny tone.

"I'll be okay as long as you promise to make it up to me."

"I know what that means." Luna blushed on the other end.

"You better." Christian blew a kiss into the phone. "I'll text you when I get home. If you want to talk dirty to me while I'm on the road, call me."

She laughed loud. "You know I will. But for now, I have to go. My next candidate will be here in fifteen minutes and I need to go pee and freshen my make up."

"Okay, bye, love."

six

"Success is the sum of small efforts, repeated day-in and day-out." Robert Collier

Christian pulled into his driveway minutes before the clock struck midnight. It had been a long, grueling day. Eleven hours on the highway, round trip, in exchange for an hour and a half visit, was always exhausting.

As one of the doors of the three-car garage rose, he drove the car into its usual spot.

Stretching and yawning, he got out of the car and went into the house. All was quiet. He had no doubt Luna was asleep. When they spoke a little over two hours ago, she told him she was going to eat and then go to bed.

Entering the kitchen, he poured a cup of lemonade and popped it in the microwave. After a long exhausting day, he enjoyed hot lemonade. When he was a boy his mother would often make it when he had a cold. It always soothed him. When Luna learned about it, she made it a habit to keep a fresh pitcher in the fridge.

He went into the bedroom. Being careful not to awake his sleeping wife, he set the cup of lemonade on the nightstand and started getting out of his clothes. He almost sat down on the bed, but quickly remembered Luna didn't think it was sanitary to sit on the bed in one's clothes unless they were fresh nightclothes or clothes put on after a shower.

Stripping down to his birthday suit, he picked up the pile of clothes, cleared his pockets, and dumped them in the clothes hamper.

He sauntered to the bathroom, turned on the rainfall shower, stepped under the soothing, hot jets of water allowing it to stream down on his head and cascade along his ripped body.

He jumped slightly when the shower door opened. He smiled when Luna joined him.

She stood on her toes, grabbed him around his neck, and nestled her nakedness against him while moving in a suggestive body caress. At the same time, a sound of desire escaped her throat.

Christian bent his head to meet her lips, drawing her against him until she was aware of his entire length. The exhaustion he felt moments earlier disappeared, replaced with passion and need.

After their intense shower, the couple returned to bed and cuddled in each other's arms.

Christian's text notifier chimed. "Who in the heck could this be? It's almost two o'clock in the morning," he complained.

"It must be urgent or a wrong number," said Luna.

Christian retrieved his phone from the nightstand. Eyeing the number, it was not one he knew. He opened the message.

"I need to see u since you can't seem to keep my name out yo mouth Mr. Hotshot lawyer. 555-555-2313 Rianna McCoy."

Christian sat up in bed and rested his back against the custom arched headboard.

"What's going on? Who is it?"

"Can you believe Rianna McCoy just texted me?"

"At freaking two o'clock in the morning!" she spouted.

"From what I've heard about her, this is how she operates. She doesn't consider others. Anyway, forget her. I'll call her in the morning when I get to the office. Let's go to sleep." He kissed her again.

"Nite, babe," Luna said and nestled under the crook of his arm.

†

Christian returned to his office from a relatively busy and trying morning in court. He was still learning about his clients, addressing their needs, and entertaining new ones.

"Attorney Black," his assistant called when he walked past.

"Yes, Beverly."

Beverly passed him the messages. Christian read the first three. All were from Rianna. He paused after reading another of her messages and then looked at Beverly.

"She's called at least a half dozen times already," Beverly stated.

"Did she say what she wanted?"

"No, only that it's urgent and she needs to see you. She said she needs to clear some things up." Beverly shook her head and frowned. "Real sassy, and if you ask me, very unladylike for someone who was a former first lady."

The phone rang again. "Good afternoon, Brachman Law Firm, Christian Black's office. How may I help you?"

"Is he there yet?"

"Excuse me? May I ask who's calling?" Beverly knew it was Rianna McCoy. As many times as the woman had called she easily recognized her snooty tone. "Ma'am, will you please hold."

Beverly didn't wait for a reply. She placed the call on hold and looked up at Christian. "It's her." She pushed her green-rimmed glasses up on her nose and pinched her lower lip with her teeth.

"I'll take it. Let me get to my office."

"Okay," she said, and then picked up the phone. "Thank you for holding. How may I help you?"

"This is Rianna McCoy....again. Is he there yet?" Irritation evident by her harsh tone.

"Mrs. McCoy, he just walked in. Can you hold for another second, please. I'll get him on the line. Thank you." Beverly put the call on hold again.

Christian went into his office, laid his briefcase on his desk, and sat on the edge of it before reaching for his phone.

"Mrs. McCoy, how may I help you? What's the urgency?"

"The urgency is you need to keep my name out *yo* mouth. I know you got my text, don't play me."

"I did see your text this morning, early this morning," he emphasized. "I'll ask you to refrain from texting me at those hours. And I have no idea what you're talking about when you say to keep your name out of my mouth."

"You know full well what I'm talkin' 'bout. Just because you're some hotshot lawyer from New York, don't mean a thing to me."

Christian remained calm. "I'm sorry you feel that way, but I can't help you if you don't tell me your concerns."

"Every time I turn around, I hear you been asking about me. If you want to know about me, anything about me, you come to me." Her tone escalated. "That lowdown ex-husband of mine will tell you anything. So will his brother and so will that uppity, think-she-so-much, ex-wife of his. That whole family got me messed up. Seems like you're fallin' right in with them. You ain't no better than that other attorney Hezekiah had, Thomas Whitfield."

"I'm sorry you're so upset, but if you'd like to schedule an appointment so we can talk about what's bothering you in more detail, we can do that. Plus, you *are* right about one thing, I do have some questions I'd like to ask you."

"Don't ask me questions about Hezekiah McCoy 'cause you might not like what I have to say about that man, my brotha."

"Tell you what," Christian said, looking at his calendar, "since you say it's urgent we talk, why don't you come in this afternoon, say around three-thirty?"

Silence filled the line for a second or two.

"Hello, Mrs. McCoy, you still there?"

"I'll see you at three-thirty," Rianna said, then abruptly ended the call.

seven

"If you don't feel it, flee from it." Paul Davis

With a close-lipped smile, Christian held the door open for Rianna and a petite, curvy woman with layers of purple box braids flowing past her bottom.

Rianna remained quiet, eyes hooded, mouth pursed. She carried, more than held, an aluminum cane as she shuffled toward his office, with a barely noticeable limp. Her companion stood on Rianna's other side, as if regarding Rianna's every step.

"Take your time," Christian cautioned. Despite the heavy tension in the air, he couldn't help but notice her physical beauty. It was easy to see why Hezekiah would have been drawn to her.

"You straight?" asked the purple-haired woman.

"Yeah, I'm good. Thanks, Tiny." The ladies entered the office with Christian taking a couple of steps ahead and extending his hand.

Christian didn't pass judgment on Rianna's friend; he was a kind-hearted individual who simply believed that the woman had a unique look. With a warm smile, he gestured towards two plush office chairs draped in elegant fabric, inviting them to take a seat.

"Please, make yourselves comfortable," he said, his rich, chocolate brown eyes glinting with hospitality. "Or, if you'd prefer, you can have a seat on the sofa near the window," he added, pointing towards the inviting piece of furniture.

Tiny batted her long faux eyebrows and flashed a toothy smile. "Wow, thanks."

Rianna and Tiny went toward the chairs. Christian stood behind each of them to assure they were comfortably seated before he walked behind his desk and sat in his chair.

Leaning back slightly in the chair and crossing one suited leg over the other, Christian could easily pass for a professional model. His smooth chocolate skin matched his deep brown eyes. The dazzling smile, closely cut beard with a low haircut, made him look close to perfection.

Tiny sat in front of him with a wide smile that looked like it had been permanently drawn on her face.

Christian refused to make eye contact with her. He'd experienced his share of flirtatious women who would gladly be intimate with him, but he would never do that to Luna. Once was enough. He told God if he would keep Luna from finding out about his moment of weakness that he would never cheat again. So far, God had protected him and so Christian honored his word, and his wife, by being faithful ever since. An attractive woman could still turn his head and make him take a second look, but that was as far as it went.

"Mrs. McCoy, I'll let you go first. I mean you did call me in the wee hours of the morning, as well as numerous times at my office. Tell me, what's going on? What's so urgent?"

"You heard what I said on the phone, Mr. Black," purposely not calling him by his professional title. "I'm sick and tired of Hezekiah McCoy trying to destroy me. Look at me! Because of him," she hollered, "the doctor said I could have a limp for the rest of my life."

With sweeping arm gestures, she continued her rant as flickers of spittle spewed out her mouth. "I don't know how long I'll be on this dang cane and having to depend on folks to do stuff for me," she said, pointing a finger at Tiny.

Tiny nodded in agreement, making a kissy face expression.

"Uh, excuse me, but who is this young lady? You didn't introduce her." Christian shifted his gaze toward Tiny.

Tiny quickly spoke up before Rianna had a chance to say a word. "I'm Tiny," she said batting her eyes, and chewing heavily on gum. "Her best friend."

Rianna looked over at her, shook her head. "Girl, you a trip," she said. Her outburst of anger seemed to simmer for a moment.

"Uh, nice to meet you, Miss....uh...Miss Tiny," Christian spoke, anticipating a last name but got none.

"Now back to what I was saying. I know you went to Hezekiah about me. And, I know you went to Stiles and that wicked first wife of his too. I can't stand her," Rianna spouted. "I can't stand none of them."

"Calm down. Look, yes, I asked Pastor Stiles about you. That I did. I also questioned your ex-husband about your marriage and your relationship. I planned to make contact with you in the next few days, but you beat me to it. To hopefully put you at ease, I wanted to meet with you and ask you to clarify some things."

"I don't have nothing to clarify," she blasted, her face hard, cruel, and pitiless. "That man is where he belongs, locked up. He don't ever need to get out. I was going up and down the highway to see his no good behind and he wouldn't even see me when I got up there. He had me so frustrated and mad that on my way back to Memphis, I had a wreck and ended up almost killing myself. Another thing, if you think he didn't do what he sitting in prison for, then you're a fool. He messed with underage girls. I don't care what he tells you or how many people he got fooled. He played them just like he played me."

"Did you have anything to do with him being charged?"

"Heck, nah!" Rianna blew up, her cheeks swelling like a blowfish. "You know what, I'm done," she screamed. "You're full of mess. You're just like all the rest of Hezekiah's circle. Come on, Tiny. Let's get out of here."

Rianna picked up her cane from off the floor. Struggling a bit, she stood up.

Tiny rushed up behind her, taking hold of Rianna's elbow to give her added support.

When Rianna started toward the door, Christian popped up and trotted to it, opening it for the ladies.

"Mrs. McCoy, I'm sorry if I upset you—that was not my intent. As for my client, I'm going to do what I can to get his conviction overturned so he can come home. In order to make that happen, I need to meet people who are or were close to him. You know, like you. If there is anything you can do to help me with that..."

"Never in a million years," she spat.

"I understand. If that's how you feel."

As she shuffled out of his office, he followed her with his gaze until she and Tiny disappeared from sight. Once they were out of view, he retreated back to his office.

A light tap sounded moments later.

"Come in," Christian announced.

"Everything okay?" Beverly asked, arms folded and a half-smile on her face. "I heard yelling. I started to come in and see if you needed my assistance."

"Thanks, but it was all good. I must say though, Rianna McCoy is a spitfire. She has her arrow pointed straight at her ex-husband's heart. When I get him released, and I feel confident I will, he's going to have to watch his back."

Beverly's smile faded and her tone grew serious. "I can tell you a litany of things she's done. Attorney Whitfield always told me she's the kind of person who he believed could physically hurt someone."

"I'm glad I know that. The more I learn about her, the more concerned I become for my client." He walked over to the window and looked out at the river. "I want to meet his first ex-wife. If you could set that up, I'd appreciate it. Tell her I want to talk to her on the suggestion of her ex-husband."

"Yes, sir. I'll get right on it. Is there anything else?"

"No, that's all," he said, looking over his shoulder. "Thanks for everything. You've helped make my acclimation at Brachman easy." He flashed a smile and turned back to gaze out the window.

His cell phone rang; the ringtone indicating it was Luna. "Hey there. Perfect timing," he said with a smile, still standing at the window.

"Why? What do you mean?"

"I just finished with a client. An interesting one at that."

"Who?" Luna queried.

"First Lady, well former First Lady Rianna McCoy. To say it was an interesting meeting will not give it justice."

"Tell me what happened," Luna insisted.

"Not now. I'll tell you about it when I get home. I have one more appointment and then I'm done for the day. You're interviewing for new employees and I'm working open cases Whitfield left behind."

"We're both getting used to being on new assignments in life. God knows what he's doing. We're going to be fine."

"Oh, no doubt. As long as we remain faithful and keep Him first," added Christian, walking from the window.

"Amen. I plan on leaving on time this evening. I want to have enough time to go home, freshen up, and grab a quick bite to eat before we have to leave for mid-week service."

"I'm glad you reminded me. I should be able to meet you at home before it's time for us to leave."

"Good. And, honey, I think I've made my decision."

"Decision? About what...the church we're going to join?"

"Yes, and I'm leaning toward Holy Rock."

"You sure about that?"

"Yes. I think that's where we belong at this stage in life. We both agreed that the congregation and even the staff seem mostly in our age range. Not to mention how diverse it is. Pastor Khalil being the son of your client should have nothing to do with where we worship."

Christian nodded and put one hand in the pocket of his slate gray Italian trousers. "I understand, sweetheart. I just don't want us to make a rash decision based on the fact it seems like the church caters to people our age. I like his style of preaching too, but I want us to be sure about whatever decision we make."

"I know, but it seems we're not on the same page. We'll talk about it some more. Maybe after tonight you'll have a better feel for where you want to be."

"That sounds good. Look, I better get going. I'll see you this evening."

"Okay, and don't be late." Luna made a kissy sound into the phone. "Love you."

"Love you more."

†

"I enjoyed it. What about you?" Luna rose from the pews and headed out of the sanctuary.

"It was good. He's a great Bible teacher. I liked the praise and worship before he started preaching. I think I could learn a lot under his teaching."

"Sounds like you're beginning to lean toward my side." Luna looped her arm inside of his as they walked toward the exit.

"I'm not saying all of that."

A short white male dressed in jeans and a striped button down shirt with shoulder length blonde dreads approached them. "Excuse me. Uh, excuse me."

Christian halted and then Luna. "Yes, how can we help you?"

"Attorney Black. Mrs. Black?"

"Yes? We're the Blacks."

"I'm Deacon Stapleton." He extended his hand toward Christian.

The men shook and then he reciprocated by shaking Luna's hand.

"If you have a few minutes, Pastor Khalil would like to meet with you. He promises not to take up much of your time."

Christian eyed Luna curiously. She smiled and spoke up first. "Of course. We'd love to meet Pastor Khalil."

"Good, well if you'll follow me to our diaconate room."

Upon entering the room, the first thing in sight was a long table with twelve chairs. A projector hung on the far end of one wall. A framed image of the Ten Commandments hung on another wall and several smaller pictures on another wall, including one of the disciples at the table with Jesus. Another plaque read, "GOD IS NO RESPECTER OF PERSONS."

"Have a seat. There's fresh coffee, caffeinated and decaf over there. Help yourself. There's also some bottled water and sodas in the fridge." He pointed at a see-through dorm size fridge in the left corner of the room. "Pastor K will join you in a minute."

"Thank you," said Christian. "You want coffee?" Christian asked Luna when Deacon Stapleton left the room. "I see some hot chocolate and tea packets over here too."

"I'll have a cup of decaf with—"

"I know how you like it," Christian finished.

"How do you think Pastor Khalil knows us? We've never introduced ourselves, and with thousands of people in attendance at each service, no way can he know us from the next person."

"I don't know. I guess we'll soon find out," Christian stated.

The door opened shortly after and Khalil strolled into the room. He'd changed from a black one button designer suit to skinny jeans, a popping cranberry polo, and signature loafers.

"Well, good afternoon Attorney and Mrs. Black. I'm Pastor Khalil McCoy."

"Hello, it's so nice to meet you, Pastor," Luna said, beaming.

Christian stood and approached Khalil as he entered. The men shook hands. "Yes, it's nice to meet you. We've visited a few times. I want to say we have enjoyed your messages and the service as a whole."

"Thank you," Khalil said. "Thank you very much."

"We located from New York several months ago. We're looking for a church home," Luna spoke up, excited.

Khalil casually strolled past Christian and took a seat a few chairs away from Luna. Christian sat in the seat next to his wife, wrapping an arm around her shoulder.

"So I heard. Welcome to Memphis. I hope you've been enjoying the city. It's full of history, life, the blues, good food and all around good ol' southern hospitality."

"That we've experienced," said Christian.

"Yes," Luna said, "so far everyone we've met has been so nice."

"Good. So, I heard you are now representing my father. Right?" Khalil eyed Christian.

"Yes, that's correct," said Christian.

Khalil pushed back from the mahogany table, clasped his hands, and rested his elbows on each chair arm.

"Is that a problem? Is something wrong?"

"No, definitely not. He's entitled to counsel, and you're entitled to represent him."

"So I get the feeling there's something on your mind. Feel free to tell me, rather us," Christian said, looking at his wife and tightening his arm around her shoulder, suddenly feeling uneasy.

Luna remained quiet, as if unsure of what was transpiring.

Khalil seemed quite nice and welcoming on one hand, but cold and distant on the other. It was a weird setting.

"I have no problem expressing myself. After all, I'm a pastor, an orator. I'm not shy by a long shot. What I want to say is I appreciate you visiting Holy Rock. We always welcome guests and new members. We're a family of sorts, a diverse group of people with one common goal— to serve God with all our hearts and souls. To praise and glorify his name."

"I agree, that's why I told my husband that I believe Holy Rock is the place for us." Luna started smiling again, and her shoulders relaxed.

Christian chimed in. "Yes, she seems to have her mind made up about us becoming part of your church family. I can understand why. You have a great ministry here."

"Again, thank you. Speaking of my ministry, I'm grateful to God for it growing by leaps and bounds. I'm glad you and your lovely wife chose to visit us." He looked at Luna and smiled a broad smile. "But I also want you to be aware that there are many wonderful places of worship throughout this city other than Holy Rock."

Christian and Luna both seemed to blink in astonished silence, taken aback at what Khalil was saying.

"I don't understand," said Luna, swallowing hard, and throwing a hand up to her face.

"All I'm saying is I suggest you continue to look for a church home. You know, make sure you're being directed by God to the right place of worship."

Christian's jaw flinched. He fully understood what Khalil was saying. *The man didn't want them at Holy Rock. Couldn't Luna see that?*

"What I'm saying is Holy Rock may not be the best place for you. I mean, you haven't been in the city long enough to know about all the great places of worship, I'm sure."

Christian's jaw kept flinching. He gripped Luna's shoulder tighter, almost causing her to jump from the slight pain.

"If you don't mind me asking, have you visited my father's church? It's a growing church. I'm sure having his lawyer on his church roll would make him feel good. Don't you think?"

"We *have* visited other churches, including your father's," Christian mouthed. His tone went ice cold and his teeth clenched. He slowly rose from his chair and then tugged gently on his wife's arm. "Honey, I think it's time for us to leave."

"Yes, you've made your point quite clear," Luna agreed, her complexion turning a shade redder now that she was fully aware of what was going on. She followed her husband's lead, and stood up.

As they turned to leave with Christian grasping his wife's hand, almost tugging her out of the room, he looked over his shoulder and said, "Thanks for being up front. It actually says a lot about you."

"I wouldn't have it any other way," Khalil said, rising from his seat and following them to the door. "Have a good day and God bless."

eight

"Call it a clan, call it a network, call it a tribe, call it a family: Whatever you call it, whoever you are, you need one." J. Howard

It had been a month since Khalil made it abundantly clear that Christian and Luna would not be welcome at Holy Rock. It still ruffled his feathers every time Christian thought about how Luna cried practically all that night. It left him feeling some type of way seeing his wife upset like that. How unchristian Khalil had behaved; certainly not like a man of God in charge.

However, unlike Luna, Christian was glad Khalil spoke his truth before they made the big mistake of joining Holy Rock.

"Have you made up your mind?" Luna asked as the couple sat in the family room munching on avocado nachos, bean dip, and chips. "I don't want to put it off any longer."

"As long as you're sure. I don't want us making the same mistake we were about to make when you wanted us to join Holy Rock," Christian said, dipping a chip into his bean dip.

"Yes, I'm sure. Like you said, God showed us where we were *not* supposed to be. I didn't see it at the time, but I definitely get it now. So, I think New Holy Rock is the place for us. We can grow there, work with their ministry programs, and we won't get lost or run over by thousands of people every Sunday. It's a smaller congregation and not to mention, I like Pastor Stiles."

"I know it wasn't where you wanted to be."

"It wasn't, but it's not about what I want, it's what God wants. Anyway, I like the intimacy of New Holy Rock and the people we've met so far."

"Good," said Christian. "I like Pastor Stiles too, and I like the layout of the services. And you're right, we'll have an opportunity to work in ministry like we did in New York. Plus, I think it'll be the perfect church for us as husband and wife, but also when we add to our family. By the way, did you hear from the adoption attorney? What's her name again?"

Some co-workers in the firm had presented Christian with a list of several top notch adoption attorneys, which he took home and shared with Luna. Luna reached out to several of them, narrowing them down to an attorney on the list named Ginny Nguyen.

When they spoke on the phone, Attorney Nguyen was knowledgeable, informative, and cordial. She carefully explained the adoption program and process to Luna and welcomed the couple to an in-person meeting.

"Her name is Ginny Nguyen," answered Luna, chuckling.

Christian flashed his charming smile. "So, have you heard from her?"

"Yes, I spoke to her earlier today. I planned to tell you. We have an appointment a week from today. I'll add it to our joint calendars."

"Good. What do we have to do?"

"We're going to fill out the application first and then we'll be able to talk more about what we're looking for. You know, whether we want to adopt an infant, toddler, older child, or siblings, overseas or here in the states. How much it can cost. You know, stuff like that."

Luna's anxious thoughts about wanting to carry a child of her own were not as invasive lately, probably because of their decision to start the adoption search. The thought of having kids, combined with the look of happiness she saw on Christian's face replaced her negative thoughts.

"Okay, I like that. I wish we could find a sister and brother. I think that would be ideal. Especially if they're still toddlers."

Luna shrugged. "That would be super. Now, come on, get up, you need to get ready for Bible study."

Christian yawned, stretched, and took another bite of his taco before he rose from his favorite recliner, a thirty-fifth birthday present from Luna.

"Are you sure you want to go to Bible study this evening?" Christian asked.

"Yes, it's only an hour. One thing about Pastor Stiles is he is not long winded. He teaches the word and sits down. We'll be in and out before you know it."

"I was just checking," said Christian.

Walking up to him, Luna kissed him on his cheek. "But if you want, we can stay home tonight. I know you've had a long day."

"Nah, I'm good. Like you said, it's only an hour."

†

"The following Sunday, Christian, Luna, Stiles, Xavier, and Fancy gathered at a charming restaurant owned by a member of the church. They savored an assortment of enticing appetizers while chatting.

"I'm glad you could join us," said Fancy. "I've been wanting to meet you, and you too, of course," she said to Luna after addressing Christian. "When you joined last Sunday I was out of town. And I don't know if Stiles, uh, Pastor Stiles," she auto-corrected, "told you that I go between New Holy Rock and Holy Rock, so you won't always see me in Sunday service."

"Yes, he told us," Luna said. "I'm glad we had a chance to meet. And Pastor Stiles, thank you for inviting us to have lunch with you and your lovely family."

Stiles nodded, chewing his food. "You're welcome."

Christian wiped his mouth with his napkin before speaking. "Yes, you've definitely made us feel welcome. You all have," he said, looking at Fancy and then Xavier.

"I hope so. I heard what happened at my son's church. I'm sorry you had such an unpleasant experience, but I hope you don't hold it against him," Fancy pleaded.

"We don't." Christian did a slight wave of his hand.

"And we don't," added Luna, "but I still thought it was a bit rude for a pastor, of all people, to turn people away from his church. I've never experienced such a thing."

Christian squeezed his wife's hand that was resting on the table top. "It's okay, sweetheart. You said yourself it was God's answered prayer. We're blessed to be in the company of you guys. I feel like we chose a place where we are accepted," he emphasized, looking around the table at each person.

"You're right." Luna looked at her husband and the couple pecked each other on the lips. "I'm sorry," she quickly apologized.

"No need for apologies. The truth is the truth," Fancy spoke up.

"She's right. God loves the truth," Stiles cosigned.

Luna smiled, relief showing on her face.

"Xavier, so you have twins, huh?" Christian deflected.

"Yes, two boys. Actually they are triplets. Their sister died at birth."

"Oh, I'm sorry," Luna said.

"Yes, definitely," said Christian.

"No need to be. God is still good. We have two healthy, rambunctious toddlers running around the crib and around New Holy Rock," Xavier said, chuckling and then placing a forkful of food into his mouth.

The table of guests laughed.

"You guys have any kids?" Xavier queried.

"No, but we are planning to adopt," Christian quickly spoke up, hoping to ward off questions about when a baby could be expected. Most people didn't mean to be offensive or rude, but some questions were not appropriate.

Christian had learned how to halt insensitive questions. It was his fault they would never have kids naturally. He lived with that truth every day, especially during times he felt his wife wanted to be pregnant with his child. Sometimes he failed to understand God and his ways. Yet, it wasn't his job to understand; but to trust and believe. He prayed the adoption process would go through quickly. There were so many children who needed good, safe, loving homes. He was confident he and Luna could be good parents.

"Adopt?" Stiles stopped eating, took a swallow of his soda, and continued. "Have you started the process?"

"Yes, we have." He looked at Luna and smiled.

"We're going to see the attorney next week," Luna said.

"I'll be praying for God's perfect will," Stiles said.

"So will I," said Fancy. "I already know the two of you are going to make the best parents."

"Thank you." Luna blushed.

"I'll give you some free pointers if you adopt little ones," Xavier offered, chuckling.

Luna giggled. "Pastor Stiles, what about you? Do you have kids?" she asked.

Stiles wiped his mouth, and took a swallow of his beverage before answering. "I have a daughter—in heaven," he said humbly.

"Oh, I'm sorry. I didn't mean to—"

Stiles raised a hand, showing his palm. "No worries, Sista Luna. God is still good. And who knows, maybe one day He'll bless me with another child if I should ever get married again." Stiles cracked a smile and started eating again.

Christian spoke up, changing the subject. "So you and my client hail from the Windy City? Right?" he said, eyeing Fancy.

"Yes," Fancy nodded, taking a bite of her seafood. "Chicago, North side. "

"If you don't mind me asking, Mrs. McCoy."

"Please, call me Fancy."

"Fancy, I was wondering if you might have known my mother, the late Caresha Perkins? They called her Carrie back then. She lived near Cabrini Green. She was about your age."

Fancy teased. "And what exactly do you think is my age?" She raised an eyebrow and smiled, halting temporarily from taking another bite of her food.

"Uh, well, I just assumed you were around the same age as my client, your ex-husband," he said, turning a shade red.

"I'm a few years his junior, but I was just messing with you," she said. "You say your mother's name is Caresha?"

"Yes, here, look at these." Christian showed her the same images he had shown Hezekiah.

"No, I don't know her. I'm sorry."

"It's okay. Thanks anyway."

"Uh, may I ask how things are going with Hezekiah? I mean, I'm just curious. Do you think you'll be able to get him an early release?" she said, worry etched in her tone.

The other table guests remained quiet and all eyes seemed to zero in on Christian.

"Yes, I feel strongly that I can get his conviction overturned. I've been looking for the so-called victims."

"Any luck?" asked Stiles.

"Yes, so far I've located one. She admitted she dated Pastor Khalil when she was a teenager," Christian said, looking at Xavier. "She said she was paid to go before the courts and lie. She said if she is called to recant her story she wants immunity. She has a kid and she doesn't want to face jail time. Also, I plan to use Attorney Whitfield's diagnose of ALS, which may have inhibited his memory and ability to fully function and represent his client."

"I see why New York didn't want to see you leave. You definitely have your stuff together," Fancy complimented.

"Why, thank you."

"And that girl you're talking about has to be Tori," Xavier spoke up.

Fancy nodded.

"Yes, that's her name," Christian said.

"She's a liar," Fancy retorted.

"I figured somebody paid her to tell that lie," Xavier snarled.

"I met with her a few days ago. She seemed sorry about what she'd done. She said she didn't think they would send him away for twelve years," explained Christian.

"I don't feel sorry for her," said Fancy. "She and that other one are why Hezekiah is where he is. Now she wants to pretend like she's sorry. I don't buy it. She just wants to save her own behind," Fancy fumed.

"It's going to be all right," Stiles piped in. "Don't let any of this get to you. Let's change the subject and enjoy the rest of our meal. I have to get my lesson plan uploaded for the upcoming week, so I'm going to have to leave shortly." Stiles took another swallow of his beverage followed by a bite of his club sandwich.

"That's right, you're a professor at the local college?"

"Yes, I am. I teach online classes."

"Well, please, don't let us hold you up," said Luna, eyeing her husband and then Stiles.

"Ohhh, no worries, you're not," Stiles said. "I still have some time."

"Christian's right. It's a perfect Sunday afternoon. Regardless, I'm sure you want to spend the remainder of your day doing whatever it is you want to do. You've fed us spiritually with the Word *and* physically with this delicious meal," Luna said, grinning. "I say enough is enough."

"I think you better listen to my wife." Christian chuckled. "Even Jesus rested on the seventh day."

nine

"Family means nobody gets left behind or forgotten."
David Stiers

Christian sat at his desk in his study, pondering over a series of questions and theories about his mother and birth father. His mother was dead; the man he always thought of as his father was dead; and he had no idea who his other family might be.

The more he scrolled social media searching for clues of any kind that might lead him to his father or his father's family, the more exhausted and frustrated he grew. He slammed a fist on his oak desk almost at the same time his office door flew open.

"Hello? Knock. Knock. You okay in here?" Luna waltzed into his office dressed in a belted, white lace booty length robe, holding a tray.

"Here you go, I thought you might like a snack. You've been in here for hours. I wish you would give it a rest." Removing a coaster from the tray, she placed the cup of peach tea on top of it. She set a saucer with three strawberry fig newton cookies next to the tea.

"Thanks, babe," Christian said, reaching for his wife.

Luna eagerly stepped up to her husband, allowing him to gather her thickness into his arms.

He held her and kissed her mid-chest. While gently easing his chair away from the desk, he pulled her onto his lap. Her breathing grew heavy and his voice grew deep as his lips devoured her face, her mouth, and her chest.

Easing her slightly off his lap without releasing his hold, he rose from the chair and hoisted her up against the black accent wall behind his desk. Having his way with her, he then guided her to his desk and sat her bottom on the desktop. Their desire rose to a feverish pitch as he pulled her firmly into the spread of his legs while his hands rose up and down the back of her spine, then buttocks.

Later that evening, after they had gone to bed, they pillow talked like they did most evenings before going to sleep. "Have you gathered any more information about your father?"

"Not really. I was thinking about doing one of those DNA test kits. At least I might find out something about my ancestors and some of my history."

"That might be a good idea."

"We'll see. I thought Hezekiah or his first wife might have known something, but that didn't work. You know I really thought he could have been my birth father."

"You don't feel like that anymore?"

"Not really."

"What changed your mind?"

"I realized it was crazy. I was just grasping at straws when there is just no connection. The man didn't know my mother. He didn't know anybody named Frankie or Bae-bruh. Nothing. I'm tired of the useless search. I'm ready to call it quits. I practically talked myself into being frustrated about a situation I have no control over. When you told me to let God handle it, that pricked my spirit because not long after you said that, I started feeling like it was time to release myself from this mental prison. All I want to do is focus on you, me and adopting kids."

Luna caressed her husband's face and then pulled herself up and kissed him on his cheek.

"Hezekiah or Horace, whatever his name, is just a guy who happened to come from Chicago the same as me. That's it. I don't know why I ever let myself think he could possibly know my father, let alone be my father. How ludicrous was that?"

"It was not ludicrous. There is nothing out of the norm about wanting to know your father. When you found out Hezekiah and his ex-wife lived in or around the same neighborhood as your mother, and they were around the same age, it raised questions. That's understandable, baby."

Luna caressed his face again as she spoke to him with love. "One thing I know is if it's for you to find him, God will show you the way."

"Yes, I know. Thank you for being my strength." Christian leaned over, kissed his wife and gathered her into his arms.

"Come on, let's say our prayers and call it a night," she said when their lips parted. "Besides, we have more important things to concentrate on. We have that meeting coming up with the adoption attorney. I have to admit, I'm a little nervous."

"No need to be nervous. What did you just tell me? Let God handle it. We only need to believe that God is already going before us and paving the way for us to grow our family. Come on, let's say our prayers."

"Agreed," Luna chimed.

They got out of bed and went down on their knees. Kneeling next to each other, they each began silently making their petitions known before God.

ten

"The family is the first essential cell of human society." Pope John XXIII

Christian grew more comfortable at Brachman with each passing day. Since joining the prestigious firm, he'd resolved and settled all the cases Attorney Whitfield left behind—except Hezekiah McCoy.

This weekend, he was flying to New York for a two-week trip to his former law firm to argue his final court case. This would be his last official business trip to the Big Apple and the official end of his time at the New York firm. While there, he hoped to see a couple of his colleagues, but not until after he finished up the big court case. It was a bittersweet feeling.

While he was spending time in New York, Luna was supposed to meet Fancy McCoy and one of Fancy's friends for a girl's retail therapy session which translated into shopping, eating, and spending lots of money. Fancy had been the one to initiate the budding friendship by asking Luna if she wanted to exchange numbers the Sunday they had lunch together.

Luna was excited about Fancy's invitation. Slowly, but surely, she was adapting to living in

Memphis. She loved the suburbs and she loved the food, especially the soul food. She enjoyed strolling along the Mississippi River with her hubby, walking on Beale Street, and listening to the music that had its origins in the city.

Christian was especially happy about the outing because he knew that Luna wasn't the easiest person to make friends. She was sweet as pie, but she was a little leery when it came to allowing people into her personal space. She'd always been that way. She admitted it was because growing up chubby, she was bullied in school. It made her reserved and quiet until she really got to know the person.

Christian remained in contact with a couple of attorneys he considered his friends from the New York firm. In Memphis, the people he'd met so far were nice and friendly but he was too busy to think about forming friendships outside of his marriage, at least for now. He had lunch with some of the other attorneys at the firm and met for business dinners with a few of them, but like him, most were busy with their own lives and professions. He was growing fond of New Holy Rock. He had started entertaining the idea of one day being appointed as a church deacon or trustee. He and Stiles were also forming a friendship which he enjoyed.

†

Before flying to New York, Christian made the drive to see Hezekiah. "I'm going out of town on business this weekend. I'll be gone for two weeks. But I want you to know that I filed your case to go before the Court of Criminal Appeals. It may take a few months for everything to move through the proper channels."

Christian looked at the notes on his tablet and then up at a frowning Hezekiah.

"I didn't mess with any underage girls," Hezekiah huffed.

"Not saying you did. Simply letting you know ahead of time that getting you released may not be an overnight process. Now, if you don't have other questions, I'm going to get out of here and head back to Memphis."

Annoyed, Hezekiah grunted and pushed himself back from the chair, rising quickly and almost in defiance, putting the guard stationed at the door on high alert.

The guard's shoulders bulged and his fists clenched as he readied himself to take a step toward Hezekiah if the need arose.

Christian raised a hand, halting the guard as a sign everything was under control. He understood Hezekiah's frustration. The man had been sitting behind prison bars for more than two years. He wanted out and Christian planned on getting his client set free.

eleven

"Family and friendships are two of the greatest facilitators of happiness." J. C. Maxwell

Christian felt a huge sense of self accomplishment, having completed a successful trip to New York, with another *not guilty* verdict He had conflicting thoughts, knowing this trial and visit ended his reign as one of the best criminal defense attorneys in New York. His next goal was to garner that same title for himself in Memphis.

Upon his return to the office, one of the first things he did was to check the papers he had filed with the Court of Appeals on behalf of Hezekiah. Everything was in order and he hoped to learn the court's decision soon.

He wrapped up things at the office and called Luna on his way out. They had a meeting with the adoption attorney.

"Luna, I'm heading to the attorney's office. I should be there in about fifteen minutes."

"Fifteen minutes? You sure? You know how bad parking can be downtown during this time of afternoon."

"I know, but I'll be there soon."

"Okay, I'm leaving now too," Luna said. "We may arrive around the same time. I'm so nervous, Christian," she admitted.

"Don't be, honey. God is in control. Okay?"

"Yes, I know, it's just that all of this is new and I'm getting anxious about the possibility of us actually adopting. I mean, what if they determine we aren't going to be good parents?"

"That's not so, and you know it. The attorney already screened us. Everything looks fine. And we have so much love to give a kid. So, stop worrying. It shows a lack of faith, baby."

"I'm trying," Luna lamented.

"See you in a bit."

"Okay, buh-bye. I love you."

"Love you, too, babe."

They ended the call and Christian pulled out of his private parking space and drove toward the street. His phone rang just as he was about to turn on the street where the adoption lawyer's office was located.

He looked at the screen. He didn't recognize the number, but there was a blue checkmark next to the word verified. And the area code he recognized as a Virginia number. The phone stopped ringing just as he was about to press the ACCEPT button. He shrugged and continued driving.

The phone rang again. The same number appeared. Frowning, he pushed the button and answered the call.

"Who the heck is this," he mumbled, not realizing he had pressed the ACCEPT button.

"Uh, I wasn't expecting that kind of greeting," the soft spoken female said.

"I'm sorry. How may I help you?" Christian asked. Her voice, however, did sound a bit familiar.

"I thought you would still have my number saved."

"Lorie? Lorie Cooper, is it you?" Christian's voice resonated with astonishment when he realized who it was. "What the hell do you want?"

"Wow, you sure know how to make a girl feel special," the woman teased. "Yep, it's me."

"Why are you calling me?" he snapped.

The woman laughed into the phone. "I thought you would be happy to hear from me. Hey, is Luna there?"

"That's no concern of yours. Now, I'm asking you one more time before I end this call. What do you want?"

"I heard you were in New York a few weeks ago. You mean to tell me that you came back to New York and you didn't bother to call your dear sweet sister-in-law? We could at least have had dinner. After all, it's been a while and remember

darling, if it wasn't for me keeping my mouth shut, your so-called perfect little marriage would be history. Possibly your career too. "
Lorie slightly laughed.

"What kind of sister are you? How can you and Luna be so different?"

The woman giggled. "You're a trip, Christianaldo. How's my sweet little sister anyway? How's her new job coming along and how do the two of you like living in the South?"

"I know you didn't call to play twenty questions, Lorie. It's been, what? Four? Five years? Frankly, I don't have time to entertain your foolishness or your threats. If you're trying to stir up trouble, you'll be sorry. I swear on my dead mother, if you do anything or say anything that could jeopardize my marriage, you'll be sorry. That's a promise."

Lorie laughed. "Who do you think you're talking to? I'm the one who holds the cards, Christianaldo. I'm the one you cheated on my poor little sister with. Hah!"

"Why are you bringing this up now? You know darn well when that happened, I didn't know you were Luna's sister. You were just one of the secretaries at the same law office. We were associates and nothing else. You know that. I hooked up with you at a freaking party that I will forever regret going to."

"Oh, but you did go and you did hook up with me. It doesn't matter that you didn't know I was Luna's sister. I can't help it if I was always the black sheep of that family. It's not my fault she and I don't have a normal sibling relationship. She calls herself such a big Christian, but she has nothing to do with me. Neither do my parents. When I got married I sent them invitations, but they didn't come. They didn't' even send a gift. Funny, huh? But it didn't matter, 'cause dude was crazy. I divorced his behind seven months later when he got arrested for manslaughter. I was done after that. Anyway, that's a whole other story. But you know what, I have to admit, I haven't been dying to see them either. I mean, it's not like they ever reach out to me. That includes Luna. She let them brainwash her too, I guess."

"Whose fault is it for your damaged relationship? Out of your own mouth you said you ran away at sixteen, got mixed up with some crazy group of druggies, got knocked up, lost the baby, went to rehab, and then nine days after you were released you went home, got high, and tried to stab your own sister. You stopped short of telling me who your family was, and I didn't ask."

"Yeah, yeah, yeah...all that is part of my past. But my oh so religious family could never forgive me. Anyway, look at me now. I'm a successful real estate broker in Virginia with my own company, with my own secretary, and my own staff of realtors. The night we hooked up at that party, think about it. It was my last week at the law firm, but I was still sharing the same social space as you and your comrades, Christianaldo. I was rubbing elbows with high powered influentials, yes indeed, the same as you. You know why, brother-in-law? Because I got it like that. My sister may be a big time executive and you may be a high powered attorney, but you're no better than me. Yes, I've made a lot of mistakes but I'm on a new path and I won't let Luna or my family, or you get in my way."

"Look, I don't know why you called, but I'm one second from ending this call and blocking you unless you tell me what it is you want."

"Oh, I was just reminiscing, thinking about how we met. You know you were looking fine as heck that night. That black Tom Ford suit you had on left a forever impression on me, and don't even get me started on that cologne - it was heavenly. I remember that scent to this day. For the life of me, I still don't understand why my sister let a fine azz man like you leave the house alone. Good for me though, because we hit it off, didn't we?" Lorie giggled.

Christian remained tight-lipped, not wanting to revisit the moment he deemed a regrettable lapse in judgment. "What's your point, Lorie?"

"My point is, I kinda miss you. And if I know my sister like I think I do, you're not getting full satisfaction from her. If you're anything like you were when we slept together, then I know your needs aren't being fully met because you were like a wild man back then. Is that why you didn't call me when you were in New York, Christianaldo? You scared of what might have happened if we were in the same space with each other again?"

"You're crazy. That was a meaningless, one-time fling, Lorie, that happened years ago. Don't try to make it something it wasn't."

Lorie broke out in laughter. "Did you say a one-time fling? Hol' up, let me refresh your memory, brotha-in-law. I think it was Rob Evans with Evans and Associates that threw that gala. Either way, I had such a good time and a little too much Bourbon, that I was going to have to call an Uber. I definitely wasn't fit to drive," Lorie laughed. "Thank God for you. You offered to drive me home instead of me calling an Uber. I thought it was so sweet of you. So I left my car at the party and accepted your offer. You were the perfect gentleman, too."

"I don't want to hear this, Lorie. I don't see your point."

Lorie continued talking, not paying attention to Christian's protests.

"You walked me to the door, and well, you know what they say. One thing led to another, and the rest is history."

Christian grew silent. This was not what he wanted or needed to be reminded of. Not now. Not ever.

"When you told me you were married, it obviously didn't make a difference to either of us, because we slept together that night and only God knows how many more times after that. I know it went on for how long, Christian? A month? Yeah, it was at least a month," she babbled. "It would have lasted longer had I not found out you were married to that so called perfect sister of mine and called things off. I guess you don't remember that either?"

"What's your point? Where is all this going?"

"The point is when I found out you were married to Luna, I was the one who told you she was my sister. If I was the bad sister like they wanted to make me out to be, I could have kept that from you and we could have kept right on sleeping together. I could have told Luna, too but I didn't. How would you have liked that, sweetie?" Lorie mocked.

Christian still said nothing, feeling ashamed of what he'd done. Here he was, after all these years, and his past had come back to haunt him. *Lord, please don't let Luna find out about this. Please God.*

"You know, I've been thinking. Are you sure you didn't know I was Luna's sister when you slept with me? You never saw pictures of me around my parents' house? Luna never mentioned me, or showed you pictures of me and her? I guess not, huh? At least that's what you wanted me to believe back then."

Christian finally spoke up. "I knew Luna had a younger sister. She said you were estranged from the family. At that time she said no one knew where you were. She said they hadn't seen you in years. And no, she didn't show me a picture of you, and no, I didn't see pictures at your parents' house. Not to mention your name last name was Cooper. Why would I even make a connection? I wouldn't," he said, his voice full of anger.

"Why am I not surprised to hear that. Anyway, the fact remains, we slept together. I liked it and you did too. So whatever."

"What do you mean, whatever? What is it you want, Lorie? Is it money to keep your mouth shut? Is this some kind of extortion call? Tell me what you want?" Christian was infuriated, biting down on his lip and balling his fist.

"I was actually thinking about coming to Memphis. I miss my big sister. It's been far too long since she and I have talked or seen each other. There's a big real estate convention in Nashville in a couple of months—I'm attending. Afterwards, I was thinking about renting a car and driving to Memphis to make amends with her, wipe our slates clean. Maybe we can have the sister relationship I've always wanted." She chuckled. "And who knows, maybe you and I can have our own little private reunion. You know, for old times' sake," she said.

"Don't you come here. Luna doesn't need that type of surprise. I know you're her sister, and as much as it pains me to admit it, I'm sure she would like to see you. Especially after all the time that's passed. But popping up here so you can destroy her by telling her about something that happened between you and me a long time ago, would be cruel. I've told you I was sorry it happened. Believe me, I wish I could turn back the hands of time, but I can't."

This time it was Lorie who said nothing.

"If you care anything about Luna, even if it's just a little bit, you wouldn't want to hurt her, Lorie. She's done nothing to deserve that. She's happy. She's settling into a new position, which she loves. As for me, I'm flourishing at this new law firm. Why can't you leave us alone and let us live our lives? What would be your reason for coming into her life now?"

"Wow, what a story." Lorie laughed loudly.

"Let it go, Lorie. Please, just let it go." Christian sighed heavily. "I asked God for forgiveness, even before I found out you were Luna's sister. Please don't hurt Luna by resurrecting the past. Leave it alone. She doesn't need this kind of stress. Neither do I. I'm begging you."

"You don't sound good begging, Christianaldo. It doesn't become you."

"Look, Lorie, all I want is to forget those things that lie behind and move forward to those things ahead."

She laughed again. "Oh, so you want to quote some scripture? Okay, let's see. Uh, I know, I know. What about this one. It goes something like this: and be sure your sin will find you out." She laughed some more. "But you know what, Christianaldo. I don't have time for this. I was bored out of my freaking mind and thought I'd have a little fun. Anyway, it was good talking to you. I may or may not be in touch soon. See ya." She laughed.

Silence infiltrated the phone line.

"Lorie? Hello? Lorie, are you there?" Christian looked at his phone and saw the call had ended. He thought about calling her back, but decided against it. He was deeply concerned about what his sister-in-law's next move would be. He couldn't shake the ominous feeling brought on by her words. *Be sure your sin will find you out.*

twelve

"God knew that it doesn't matter how your children get to your family. It just matters that they get there." K. Mortenson

"I've received your background checks. I'm waiting on your financial history to come back," Attorney Nguyen informed the excited couple. "Everything looks promising. Today, I'd like to learn more about your preferences," Nguyen said, pushing her black rimmed designer eyeglasses up on her moon shaped face.

Luna spoke up, briefly eyeing Christian as if she was seeking his approval. "We'd like a younger child. Preferably a little girl. If an infant is available that will be even better."

Christian smiled and nodded in agreement. "We've also talked about adopting siblings, preferably a girl and a boy, but the bottom line is, Attorney Nguyen, we just want healthy little kids, someone we can love, who can bless us and who we can be loving parents to."

The attorney smiled. "That is wonderful. Now, let me go over some things about adoption with you. There are generally four options when it comes to adoption. You have foster, domestic, international, and kinship."

"Excuse me," Luna spoke up, "remember, we're not interested in international adoption."

"Yes, I remember. I just want to make sure you understand the differences. For instance, with foster care adoptions, your selection of children will come from the state's foster care system. The average age of children in foster care waiting for adoption is about seven years old."

Luna looked at Christian. He grabbed hold of her hand and covered it in his.

"Next, there is private adoption or what we sometimes call domestic adoption. This kind of adoption allows the adoptive parents to get the age, gender, and race of the child they desire. This is more popular for those who want infants."

"I like the sound of private adoption," Luna spoke up, squeezing Christian's hand.

Attorney Nguyen smiled, made a quick note, and continued talking. "In a private adoption, you may be able to choose between having an open adoption or a closed adoption. An open adoption is where the adoptive parents meet the birth parents and keep an open line of contact with the birth family. In a closed adoption, neither party knows much, if anything, about each other."

"I don't want the birth parents to know us. I think it can cause confusion and conflict when the child gets older." Christian said, and Luna agreed.

"That can be arranged," Attorney Nguyen assured. "There is also kinship adoption. This is when you adopt a family member."

Luna shook her head. "That doesn't fit us."

"Last, there is international adoption which you've already said you are not interested in."

"Right, I believe private adoption is the best way for us," Christian reinforced. He looked at Luna and lovingly squeezed her hand. "Right, honey?"

"Right," Luna said, "but we don't want to dismiss adopting an older child from foster care—it's just not our first choice."

"Okay." Attorney Nguyen entered something into her computer again.

"What kind of costs are we looking at?" Christian queried further.

"The average cost to adopt through an agency is around forty-thousand."

"How long does it usually take?" asked Luna.

"Anywhere from several months to a year or more." She began entering something into her computer again and then looked up at the couple once she was done.

"The next thing that will take place is a home visit. After that is completed, we can start accepting referrals until you find the child or children for you." Attorney Nguyen smiled.

Christian and Luna left Attorney Nguyen's office full of excitement, expectation, and hope.

"Christian, can you believe we're actually going to do this? We're going to adopt. Every time we talk to Attorney Nguyen, I feel like we're on the verge of our life changing forever."

"Yes, God is going to grant us the desires of our hearts. Soon we're going to hear little feet running through the house. I can't wait," he said as they strolled out of the office building hand in hand.

Stepping outside, they paused in front of the three story structure. "I have to run back by the office and finish up a few things," Luna said.

"But I thought you were done for the day."

"I did too, but before I left, something came up and I need to tend to it. It shouldn't take long. Maybe an hour, no more than that, and I'll be right home. I promise."

Christian's eyebrows raised. "Okay. Do you want me to pick up something on my way home? I don't feel like cooking anything tonight. I know you probably don't either, especially since your day still isn't over," Christian empathized. "We have two orders of "Hello Fresh" delivery in the fridge, if you want that."

"Nah, that means still having to cook, and I'm with you, I don't want to do anything when I get home but take a shower, eat, and go to bed."

"Okay, so what do you want me to pick up?"

"What about something from Silver Caboose?"

"Silver Caboose is good with me. I like their food, and it's close to the house. What do you want?"

"Get me their Reuben sandwich on marble rye with everything on it and a slice of blackberry cobbler."

Luna loved food which was evident in her heavy, wide hips, 44DDD breasts and large shapely legs. As much as she ate, it was surprising she didn't weigh more than her present 198 pounds. She found Southern food tempting and tasty. Sometimes she didn't think she could get enough of the tantalizing cuisine.

Christian was not the slightest bit perturbed by his wife's curvaceous figure. Rather, he cherished and adored her voluptuousness.

"Where did you say you parked?"

"On Second Street," she said.

"Okay, I'll walk you to your car."

"No, baby. I'll be fine. I'm just around the corner at the end of the block."

"Okay, well I'll see you in a bit." He bowed his head toward hers as she stood on tiptoes to meet his thick, wet, luscious lips.

"Love you," he said when their lips parted.

"Love you more."

thirteen

"The power of prayer doesn't come from the words we say, but from the One who hears them."
Vanderheiden

Christian paced the wide-plank maple hardwoods while looking at his phone. It was almost eight o'clock and Luna still hadn't made it home. He had tried calling her several times since six o'clock. Whatever she had going on at the office should have been over with, especially at this hour. He called the office phone line as well. It went to the department's voicemail.

Calling her again, her phone rang until her voicemail came on—again. He didn't leave a message the past few times, but this time, he was almost in a panic so he left one.

"Luna, where are you? It's after eight o'clock." He swore, something he rarely did. "Why won't you answer my texts or calls? I know you can't still be working. Honey, please, just call me. I need to know you're okay. You've got me worried."

Another half hour passed. Luna still wasn't home. He called again. "If I don't hear from you in the next fifteen minutes, I'm calling the police, Luna," he said nervously, still pacing around the house.

†

"Christian, my brother, we are praying for Sista Luna's safe return," Stiles said, trying to console his new friend and church member. He placed a hand on Christian's shoulder as he spoke. "I know you're scared but you have to let the police do their job. They're going to find her and bring her home safely. We just need to keep the faith."

"I know, Pastor and believe me, I'm trying to keep the faith," Christian cried.

Fancy appeared from Christian's guest bathroom. "She's coming home. Don't you worry. Now, are you sure there's nothing we can do for you? You still haven't eaten?"

Christian shook his head. "No, I'm not hungry."

"You need to keep up your strength, Christian. I don't want Luna coming home and finding you all skinny and scrawny. She'll think we didn't take care of you," Fancy tried to tease and sound upbeat. It didn't work.

"I'm good. Thanks for your concern, Sista McCoy, but I just don't have an appetite."

"I told you about that—call me Fancy. We're not just church friends; your wife is becoming like a daughter to me. I know the good Lord is going to bring her home safely. I just know it," Fancy said, walking up to Christian and taking a seat next to him on the sofa. She wrapped an arm around him and pulled him close. Like she would do her own sons, she wrapped her hand around his head and pulled him to her shoulder, kissing him affectionately on the crown of his head.

"There's plenty of food in the kitchen. Ever since the congregation heard about Luna's disappearance, the church phones haven't stopped ringing. Folks have been calling wanting to know what they could do. That food is from many of our members. The Kitchen Ministry put it together. Everything is already cooked, labeled, and ready to heat and eat."

Christian remained quiet, almost as if he hadn't heard a word Fancy said.

"Just know, like Pastor Stiles said, we're here for you. We're praying and we won't stop until they bring Luna home. I'm going to join the search team tomorrow."

"So am I," said Stiles. "I know we have at least fifty, maybe more, New Holy Rock members who have already signed the volunteer sheet to join the search."

Christian looked up at Stiles, tears in his eyes. "I don't know how to thank you."

"No need. That's what God's folks are supposed to do; support one another. The word of God in Isaiah forty-three and two says, when you pass through the waters, I will be with you; and through the rivers, they shall not overwhelm you; when you walk through fire you shall not be burned, and the flame shall not consume you. Believe that, my brother. Wherever Luna is, God's got her. He's got you, too. So do we."

Christian swiftly wiped tears away and bowed his head, shying away from Fancy and Stiles' stares. He was appreciative for them rushing over when they heard about Luna's disappearance.

Since the story aired three days ago, the local news stations had been replaying it repeatedly, hoping someone would come forward with clues, but so far there had not been anything about her possible whereabouts.

The afternoon they left the attorney's office was the last time he had seen or heard from his wife. He beat up on himself for not insisting on walking her to her car that afternoon. What had he been thinking?

The doorbell rang.

"I'll get it," Fancy said, popped up from the sofa, and hurried to the front door.

Christian rose shortly after.

"Thank you, thank you so much. I'll tell him. Good night," she said, closing the door.

Fancy turned and almost bumped head on into Christian's chest. His quick reflexes caught the two bags of food containers she held.

"Whoa," he said, "let me get those." He removed both bags from her hands.

"This is from your neighbors next door. He said to tell you that he and his wife are praying that the police will find Luna and the person who took her."

Christian nodded and walked back up the hallway and into the kitchen. Like a robot, he placed the bags on top of the island and began removing the contents. There was a glass bowl of roast with gravy, potatoes, and carrots; a huge salad, a bowl of green beans; a dish of cobbler and a pan of cornbread.

"Looks delicious," said Fancy, walking up beside Christian, licking her lips.

Stiles appeared. "One thing for sure, you won't go hungry, not for a very long time." He patted Christian on his shoulder and walked over to Fancy.

"I think it's about time we let this man get some rest."

Fancy agreed. "Stiles is right; you need to eat and you need to rest. But I want to put some of this food away first."

"You don't have to do that," said Christian. "I'll do it later."

"No, it won't take but a minute." Fancy insisted, and started putting food away. "You need to do like Stiles said, get some rest."

"I don't know if I can. My mind is all over the place. Where could she be?"

"Look, I know this is difficult, and it may be easy for me to say, but you've got to turn this thing over to God. You need your strength mentally and physically. Tomorrow is going to be another long and exhausting day. We have miles to cover. It's going to take all the energy you can muster."

"I know," mumbled Christian. "No one or nothing will stop me from searching for my wife....not until I find her." He placed his head in his hands and then rubbed his forehead back and forth.

Fancy continued putting away the food. The double door stainless steel refrigerator was quickly filling up with donations. The Blacks may have been a new presence in the city but already their neighbors, church family, coworkers, and strangers, were showing them love and sending up prayers for Luna.

"I've got everything put away and the kitchen is all clean," she said about twenty minutes later. "You ready?" she turned and asked Stiles who returned in the house after having taken out the trash.

"Yes, I'm ready." The three of them walked out of the kitchen, up the hallway, to the front door.

Fancy extended her arms and embraced Christian in a tight hug. "She's coming home safe and sound. Watch what I tell you," she whispered.

Christian opened the front door but remained quiet.

Stiles stepped up and gave him a hug. "God bless you, my brother. Good night."

"Good night. Thanks again for everything. Both of you have been lifesavers."

Fancy stopped on the front porch. "What about her parents?" she asked.

"They're flying in tomorrow afternoon. I tried talking them out of coming right now, but that's because I thought she would have been home by now."

"I can't say I blame them. I'd be here in a heartbeat too if it was one of my kids," Fancy said.

"You're right," Christian said.

"If you need us to pick them up from the airport or transport them anywhere, let me or Fancy know," Stiles offered.

"Yes, anything, anything at all we can do, let us know." Fancy added as she and Stiles walked up the paved walk toward Stiles' car.

Christian remained at the front door, watching them until they backed out of the driveway and disappeared up the street.

Looking up at the sky, he allowed a round of salty tears to freely flow down his stubby face and cheeks. "God, let Luna be safe. Let her be alive. Bring her home to me." He stood outside for several minutes before going back inside the empty house.

Had this been the right move? As rowdy and wild as New York could be, he had never felt unsafe and Luna had never expressed any real concern about her safety in New York either. They freely came and went, enjoying their lives and careers. Now they come to Memphis and this happens.

Luna had felt uneasy about relocating, but that was mostly because she was concerned about him, a Black man in the South. In the end, she accepted her new position and they moved. They began looking forward to their new lives in Memphis. Meeting new people, trying new things, seeing new sights, and most of all, preparing to start a family. What was he going to do now? He prayed harder; he couldn't see his life without Luna.

fourteen

"Prayer does make a difference—a life-changing, mind-blowing, earth-rattling difference." TerKeurst

The disappearance of pharmaceutical executive Luna Black made headlines across the mid-south, sparking widespread concern. However, today's search was abruptly terminated due to an approaching monstrous storm with punishing straight line winds and hail that threatened to unleash its wrath upon the city. The heavens had already darkened to a menacing gray hue, and it was barely past midday.

"I can't believe they're calling off the search," Christian complained.

"I know, but MPD wants to make sure the search party makes it home safely before the storm moves in," Stiles said.

"That's why I need to be out there looking for my wife!" Christian's temper flared. He struck a wooden beam along the search perimeter with his foot.

"Try to calm down. Getting yourself upset like this is not good," Fancy cautioned, watching Christian's outburst.

"I don't want to hear what's good or not good for me! Don't you understand, nothing will be good until my wife comes home!"

Stiles and Fancy planted themselves on each side of Christian, wrapping their arms around the broken man.

Luna's parents were just as upset as Christian. The retired couple, like any parents, were besides themselves with worry.

"We're going to find her," Stiles continued to reassure them all when they arrived at Christian's home after a long, exhausting, futile search.

†

Luna's mother jumped hearing the deafening boom of thunder that echoed like a massive explosion outside. Winds raged with ferocity, causing the entire house to tremble. Trees whipped back and forth, some bending to the brink of breaking, sending twigs and branches careening across the streets in Christian's neighborhood. The rain pounded relentlessly against the windows, as if it were trying to break through with sheer force.

"Oh, God, I can't imagine my baby being out there all alone and frightened. Lord only knows what's happened to her. Oh, Lord, where is she?" Luna's mother cried.

Her husband gathered her in his arms and held her close. "*Shhh*, don't cry. They're going to find her. They're going to bring her back," Luna's father tried to soothe his wife. "You'll see. God is going to bring our sweet girl back to us."

Christian, drained, eyes red and swollen from lack of sleep, barely nodded. His mind was all over the place. He hadn't shaved since Luna's disappearance and had barely eaten the past few days. Going into the law office or going to see Hezekiah McCoy was out of the question. He could not concentrate on anything but finding his wife. Until she came home, no one and nothing else mattered.

The day before, Luna's car was found parked on a dead-end street in Horn Lake, Mississippi. There was extensive front end damage. Her empty purse and her keys were inside the car, along with a teal blazer she had on the day of her disappearance.

Later that night, alone in his bedroom, Christian got on his knees and cried out to God. When he finished praying, and was lying in bed, he looked over to where Luna would normally be laying. Reaching over, he ran his hand up and down the space.

From out of nowhere, he recalled something one of the search party volunteers said to him on the first day of the search: "I'm sorry to hear about your wife. Me, my wife and my kids came to help search for her." Before walking away, the volunteer told Christian, "This may sound cold and heartless, but welcome to Memphis."

fifteen

Heal your soul. The healing of your body and mind will follow." Unknown

Christian loomed over Luna's hospital bed, unkempt and weary, with slumped shoulders, reflecting both defeat and gratitude that his wife had been found alive. Tears blurred his vision as he gazed upon her swollen and heavily battered form, her breathing shallow and erratic as she drifted in and out of consciousness.

Luna was connected to an IV filled with medication that slowly eased her pain. Christian tenderly stroked her matted hair and moistened her dry, cracked lips with Vaseline.

It was a miracle that Luna was found at all. She was discovered by a couple jogging along the running trails near Fuller Park in South Memphis. They stumbled upon a barely conscious Luna, half-naked, bruised up, and seemingly left to die amidst dense shrubs and forests of the South Memphis park.

Luna was unable to tell the police or Christian details of what had happened. An examination showed she had a concussion, cracked ribs, and a fractured elbow. She had been viciously beaten and sexually assaulted.

"We're going to find who did this to you, baby," Christian cried, leaning down and whispering into his wife's ear. "Don't you worry. I'm here. I'm not going anywhere." He kissed her swollen parched lips, being extra gentle. Crusts of blood was still on her nose, face and on different parts of her body.

"Excuse me," the ICU nurse said, walking up quietly behind Christian. "I'm sorry, sir, but you have to leave. Visitation resumes at two," she explained, stepping up and checking Luna's vitals.

"Just a couple of more minutes," he pleaded, rubbing his stubbled chin while waiting on the nurse to complete her tasks.

"Okay, but a couple of minutes only."

"Thank you," he whispered.

When she was finished checking Luna's vitals, Christian stepped back to his wife's bedside. He gently laid his hand on top of hers.

"I have to leave, but I'll be back, sweetheart. I promise. You hang in there. You've got to come back to me. We have babies to adopt, remember," he said, trying to keep back his tears but found it almost impossible. He turned slowly, looked back over his shoulder, and then left out of the ICU room.

On the drive home to freshen up, a call came in. His first thought was to ignore it, but as if on impulse, he pressed the button and answered the call.

"You have a call from a Tennessee inmate. If you accept this call you will incur charges in the amount of one dollar per minute. Press one if you accept the call and charges. Press two or hang up if you do not accept this call."

Christian reluctantly accepted the call.

"Hello."

"Hello there, Black," Hezekiah said. "How are you?"

"Look, right now I have a lot going on. I told you, my wife is missing," he said, his voice elevating. "All I can tell you is I'm still waiting to hear from the high court. There's nothing more to tell you."

"Actually, I wasn't calling about my case. You've done a pretty good job keeping me informed about that. I was calling to tell you how sorry I am to hear about your wife. I saw on the news they found her. How is she?"

Taking a moment before answering, Christian exhaled and then slowly spoke. "Thanks for your concern. She's pretty banged up, but doctors expect her to survive. She's in ICU right now."

"I'm so sorry to hear that. Just know I'm praying for her and for you. Some of the guys in my prison worship group are praying too. You just keep the faith."

"Thanks. That means a lot. And look, know that I'll be in touch as soon as I hear something. In the meantime, feel free to call me like you did today. If I don't answer, well, it means I am more than likely at the hospital with my wife. I hope you understand."

"I do. Take care and I'm praying for you, my brother."

✝

Three weeks after Luna's brutal assault and kidnapping, she was out of the hospital and back at home but her recovery was far from complete. While her physical injuries were healing, her mental state remained in turmoil. Luna was not the same person she had been before the attack. She had become withdrawn and reticent, plagued by restless nights filled with nightmares. Even though her memories were shattered, she still struggled to piece together what had happened during that fateful period.

"We had just left the adoption attorney. When I got to my car, I remember hearing a man's voice coming from behind me or somewhere close. He sounded like he may have had an accent, maybe like he was Hispanic, but I can't be sure. He told me not to scream, not to turn around, and not to say a word or he would kill me. He had a gun or a knife poked at the back of my neck. That's all I remember. I don't know if I got in my car and drove, or if he drove. I don't remember if there was someone with him. I'm trying, but I can't remember." She began to cry.

"Honey, please don't do this. Let it go for now. It'll come back to you soon enough."

Christian struggled to communicate with his wife after her rescue. She resisted his touch and refused to share the same bed. He empathized with her, but a part of him felt neglected. It wasn't about sexual intimacy; he understood her hesitation in that regard. But rather, their bond seemed broken, and her trust in him had faded. He made an effort to understand her thoughts and to make sure he was patient. But he couldn't shake these emotions. Whoever had harmed his wife, he harbored a deep desire for their ultimate retribution.

Later that evening he prepared dinner for the two of them. "Hey, babe, how are you feeling? I brought you dinner," he said, carefully entering the bedroom holding a tray of food and a small bouquet of red roses with strands of eucalyptus trailing throughout.

"The flowers are beautiful. Luna eased upright, resting her back against the headboard. "Thank you," she whispered, reaching for the tray and placing it over her legs.

Minutes after she finished eating, she complained of feeling lightheaded and sick to the stomach. Right after telling this to Christian, her dinner came up, soiling her clothes and the bed coverings.

"I'm so sorry," she cried, wiping away spittle and vomit from her mouth with the back of her hand.

"It's okay." Christian ran into the linen closet and returned with a package of wet wipes and several towels. "Come on, let's get you out of this mess," he said lovingly. "You probably ate too fast."

Luna moaned, slowly got out of bed, and removed her soiled clothing. After taking a warm bath, she returned to bed where she saw Christian had changed the linens and laid out a fresh clean gown for her.

sixteen

"In family life, love is the oil that eases friction, the cement that binds closer together, and the music that brings harmony." Burrows

"I still don't think it was necessary to make all this fuss," Luna complained at the doctor's office. "I told you, I feel better. I think it was just a stomach bug, plus you know I get queasy sometimes when I think about what happened. It's going to take some time before I feel like I'm back to normal again. That's what the therapist told me, and I agree. I don't see why you insisted that I see a doctor."

"I know, sweetheart, but it's not normal to be physically ill almost every day like you are. It's been almost two months since the assault. And before you get upset, I'm not saying you should be over what happened. I don't mean that at all. Matter of fact, I'm saying just the opposite. Your physical injuries and bruises are almost gone, but you're still wrestling with a lot mentally and emotionally. I can't blame you, especially since we haven't found out who did this to you."

"I thought about that too. You know I've always dealt with gastritis and stomach issues, especially when I get stressed or overly anxious," Luna cosigned. "I just wish they could find who did it. I think that will make it all better. Tomorrow will be my first day back in the office. I need to have it together, Christian."

"See, that's what I'm talking about. Look at how stressed you are. You're getting yourself all worked up and worried about going back to work when there's no rush. You know we're straight financially. But if you insist on working, why don't you start working from home until you feel like you're ready to go back to the office full time."

"I could do that, but I think it's time I go back to the office, even if it's only a couple of days a week. I can't keep hiding from life and living."

Sitting on the exam table, Luna twisted her hands together, warding off a fresh mounting bout of anxiety.

"You okay? You're trembling." Christian picked up the small trash can in the exam room, walked up and stood next to his wife. "Here, in case you have to throw up." He placed the trash can next to her.

Luna nodded.

Taking hold of her hands, he massaged them and then kissed her cheek.

"I need to deal with what happened because no matter how bad I want it to, it's not going to go away, Christian. I'm trying to get over it by seeing a therapist and not keeping my feelings bottled up inside."

"You're doing great," Christian encouraged.

"Yeah, but maybe I would get better even faster if they could find out who attacked me. When I saw the video they captured near my car, I couldn't tell who the person was either. All I saw was he had on sunglasses with dark blue jacket and jeans, and a hoodie pulled over his head. They've shown the clip on news channels over and over, and still no one has come forward. At least not anyone with any clues that checked out."

The door opened and the doctor appeared. "Well, Mrs. Black. Oh, and Mr. Black," the doctor said, eyeing each of them with a slight smile. "Your tests came back normal, all except one."

Luna's eyes widened and Christian held his wife close, squeezing her hands in his, afraid of the news the doctor was about to share.

Christian prayed that it wasn't bad news. *God, please let my wife be all right. Please, God.*

"What is it, Doctor? What is it that we need to know?" Christian urged.

"Yes, just say it," Luna said, tears already forming in her eyes at the thought of what dreadful news the doctor was about to share.

"Mr. and Mrs. Black...congratulations, you are going to be parents."

Words from the Author

As I continue to write this short story series, I find myself continually captivated by new revelations. Though I had hoped for a positive turn between the McCoys and the Grahams, life always has a way of throwing curveballs that remind me of the unpredictability of real life. Even when everything seems to be going well, unexpected events can arise and change the course of everything.

The characters in this storybook are not unlike us in their struggles and challenges. While they exist in a fictional world, many of their experiences mirror those that so many of us face in our daily lives.

It is true, we don't always receive the cards of life we had hoped for, but I believe that maintaining faith in a higher power, as well as positive thinking and self-affirmations, can help us overcome obstacles and live our best lives. Though we may not be able to conquer every mountain, we can learn from the characters in this series and find ways to navigate around them or even conquer them altogether.

More Perfect Stories About Imperfect People
Like You...and Me

Adverse City Series
The Real Housewives of Adverse City 1
The Real Housewives of Adverse City 2
The Real Housewives of Adverse City 3
The Real Housewives of Adverse City 4

Beautiful Ugly 2-book series
Beautiful Ugly
True Beauty

Young Adult Titles
House of Cars
Life of Payne
The Lollipop Girl

Standalone Novels
Always Now and Forever Love Hurts
Into Each Life
Sinsatiable
What's Blood Got To Do With It?
Only In My Dreams
The House Husband
Cross Road
The Truth About Sista Brianna
Forever Ain't Enough

Anthologies
Bended Knees
Weary to Will
Learning to Love Me
Show A Little Love 1

Show A Little Love 2

A Christian's Perspective:
Journey Through Grief

How to Live Your Life Like It's Golden

Journals
Journal Your Way Through It
Sister Sister Book Log Journal

Contact information
www.sheliaebell.net
www.sheliawritesbooks.com
sheliawritesbooks@yahoo.com
www.facebook.com/sheliawritesbooks
@sheliaebell (Twitter & Instagram)

Join my mailing list for literary updates and new book release information
www.sheliawritesbooks.com

If you enjoyed this book or any of my books, please go to your favorite review site and leave a positive review!

Other links to my books
bit.ly/sheliaebell
bit.ly/sheliabn
bit.ly/sheliaebell
www.sheliawritesbooks.com

#iwriteforfilmandtv
#iwritebestsellers
#iwritepageturners
#iwritenewyorktimesbestsellers
#iamgodsamazinggirl

Perfect Stories About Imperfect People Like You ...and Me!